VOLUME ONE

BOOK FIVE

THE ORISHA OF SAHAEL

BY

DWAYNE ANTHONY MADRY

Printed in the United States of America

First Printing, 2024

ISBN 978-1-963089-04-2

Cover Design by JessHavok

www.SAHAEL.com

Intoduction into Sahael

As Oadira strives to overcome the trials and obstacles to reclaim Sahael as her home and ensure the safety of her children and people, she is unexpectedly faced with another task. The one who originally sent her to Sahael in the first place appears, presenting her with a new challenge that she must undertake to truly set things right. This task adds a new layer of complexity to Oadira's journey, testing her resolve and pushing her Orishan gifts to their limits.

Despite the unexpected twist, Oadira must find the strength and determination to confront this new challenge head-on, knowing that the fate of Sahael, her people, and Aarde itself hangs in the balance. With the support of her family and the guidance of the ancient flame, Oadira embraces this new task with courage and determination, determined to fulfill her destiny and secure a brighter future for all.

CHAPTER CONTENTS

CHAPTER I

A MARULA BRANCH

The Society of Secrets, Western Aarde

Oadira stood in the ruined city of Synagogue, another way station on her journey back to Sahael. During her 50 years of life, Oadira had seen genocide, slavery, murder, rape, opulence, wealth, and abundance.

The contradictions didn't end there.

Her entire existence had been a tug of war between destiny and free will. She had been called to unite a people and protect the world, but her desires for peace and quiet stood in contrast to the fights and wars she had at times led.

She started out as a slave worth only what her breeding rights would afford her owner. From there she had been a runaway slave, became a queen, fought in a war, traveled to mystical lands, endured spiritual trials, and been named empress of a hidden realm.

And now she stood on the steps of a rebuilt pillared temple with her husband, Ozias, their three adult sons and the fourth only

16 years old, flanked by her confidante and friend Lyshyla. In front of them, basking in the sun like holy priests who preferred darkness, stood a foreign Educator and three bastard daughters of Sahael. Instead of helping Oadira's family on their quest to reunite the oppressed people and bring peace to Aarde, they were telling her that once again her journey to reestablish a sacred kingdom would be impeded by the selfish desires of someone else.

Prophecies spoke of one thing, while politics spoke of another. Oadira had very little patience left for either.

"What do you mean, 'the price will be high?'" Oadira asked Educator Nortan, a tall, older gentleman with coarse white hair and a dark wrinkled face. He wore fine robes of red, gold, and green. Behind him stood three of the four Bastard Daughters of the Four Bloodlines, royal women of Sahael exiled as babies because of the indiscretions of their fathers. They were beautiful, ebony-skinned princesses dressed in similar robes to the educator, with voices that sounded almost identical one to the next.

And they had helped Natas overthrow Sahael, leading to the murder of millions. They had been betrayed by the demon-man afterward, but that did nothing to quelch Oadira's indignation.

They were traitors, and she had little desire beyond making them pay for the genocide of so many. They may not have wielded the swords themselves, but they had opened the gate and let in the wolf to do his carnage.

"As I said," Educator Nortan replied after a pause. "We have the means to get you to Sahael to fulfill your prophesied duty. But we require something in return. We knew the words of the ancients ourselves and have known that eventually a queen of Sahael would arrive seeking aid. The daughters Sy, Ky, Ny, and Fy are prepared to serve you."

"What are you hoping for in return?" Oadira asked with Lyshyla by her side.

"A Marula branch from the Chosen and Ancient Bloodlines…for Sahael to allow the Society of Secrets the opportunity to return home," Educator Nortan said.

"What does that mean?" Oadira asked as she rolled her eyes.

"Marriage," Educator Nortan said.

Lyshyla gasped. Ozias' neck tightened.

"What?" Oadira yelled.

First Leader Sy stepped forward, standing directly in front of Ozias and Oadira, a few feet away from their faces. "You have three fine-looking sons over the age of eighteen. An agreement of betrothal between them and my sisters and I would secure not only an alliance but would make sure the Bastards of Royalty have a place in Sahael."

Oadira looked Sy directly in the eyes. "That cannot and will not happen! My boys are not going to be traded off for a favor! My entire youth was spent waiting for such a fate, until I fled and found my true love on my own. My sons will have the same chance. And Onika is not yet 17 years old. My family and I will find our own way out of this place and discover a different way to Sahael without your help!"

Her words echoed through the plaza, drawing the attention of several passing merchants and a group of stone masons working on a nearby building.

Educator Nortan stepped forward and nodded. "The two of you, Queen Oadira and King Ozias, share the same lineage; you and your family may be purebloods but only of the Orishan bloodline. Second Leader Ky is also part of the pureblood; she shares the Yoruban bloodline. Then there's Ny who also shares part of the Hausan. Finally, Fourth Leader Fy, who has just arrived from Naharis's realm with Davú Denos of the Demir, is the last who shares a part of the pure Demirrian bloodline."

Up the steps walked a woman obviously related to the bastard sisters. Fy shared their same characteristics and mannerisms, distinguished by her turquoise Kingman-colored eyebrows and eyes. She hugged her sisters, and after a brief recap, stepped next to Ny.

"I am sorry I was not present for your welcome," Fy said.

"Some welcome," Oxum mumbled. His brothers chuckled quietly.

"Please," Nortan said, arms opening wide. "Let us enter the Citadel of Synagogue and eat. I can tell you are all tired from your journey. Allow us to show you some hospitality."

Oadira had no desire to follow them anywhere, but her hunger and fatigue could not be ignored. Since arriving in Western Aarde through the Nairohenge Gate, her, Ozias, and their sons had been weakened, losing much of their natural power to create weapons of light and commune with the elements. Plus, their recent fight with the assassins had led to her three oldest boys all being drugged by poisoned darts. Fighting at this time would not be a sound strategy. Best to eat and rest before planning their next move.

"We will go with you, so long as you have your word we will be safe," Oadira said.

Lyshyla stepped close to Educator Nortan. "It would be against the laws of our ancestors for them to offer respite as a feint for attack." She paused, staring at her fellow Educator. "But obviously, they've betrayed before."

Nortan smiled, his white teeth standing in contrast to his dark brown skin. "We would not think of it. Our desire is for our people to become one through marriage, not to sever relationships further."

After Educator Nortan finished speaking, they were escorted to the interior of Synagogue. Tall ceilings held up by columns of woodstone stared down on them, while colorful tapestries depicting different historical moments hung from bars above. Fires burned on elevated stands adding light to the otherwise drab setting. Servants rushed in roasted chickens and platters of tubers and herbs. Oadira and family ate to their fill, glad for a respite from walking, hiding, and fighting.

"You'll need some time to think over what Educator Nortan has said," First Leader Sy said as she took a drink of fruit wine. "In the meantime, the Scions will guide you to your quarters until you're requested once more."

The Scions led the family to a series of stone buildings that had been rebuilt much like the citadel. The rooms were comfortable, but nothing like what they had enjoyed in Nier's Realm or even the palace of Iceoth. The entire city, while obviously once beautiful and regal, was now in a state of reconstruction without resources. People on the street still held their heads high in memory of better days past, but now lived in a situation where everything from food to building material was scarce.

"This is completely unexpected," Oadira said as she stood on a balcony overlooking the market below. She took several deep breaths to calm herself.

"They're doing what's needed to save their people and society," Lyshyla said from a patched sofa beside a table with scratches across the wooden veneer. Ozias sat at the table, brooding silently. "This people will have a role to play if Sahael is to be restored," Lyshyla continued. "After the births of you and your three cousins, the union of the tribes from all over Aarde was triggered. When Sahael was invaded by Lord Commander Natas and the Narsans, those same tribes were scattered and lost. The

Society of Secrets is one of the bloodlines that was created out of the selfishness of men and women."

"So, what you're saying is Educator Nortan is right?" Ozias asked. He stared at the table; hands clenched in front of his face. "We should trade our sons for a way into Sahael?"

Lyshyla shook her head. "I'm saying that if you want to get to Sahael and help with the first gathering, what Educator Nortan has proposed makes complete sense. They're one of the twelve tribes who are a part of the first gathering, created by the negligence of the Chosen and Ancient Bloodlines. The brothers of your father and mother lived loosely, spreading their seed all over Alkebulan. Their immaturity forced Solomon to act and get involved as he reached out to us to help remedy this situation; their sins have fallen upon you to rectify their mistakes, and this is how you'll do it."

"The sins of the bloodline fall upon others to fix the mistakes of the past?" Oadira asked, stomping her foot. "So, it falls upon my bloodline to resolve their past failures and mistakes? How is that fair?"

"Such is the responsibility of your bloodline," Lyshyla answered. "It requires more out of you than you could ever imagine. It's as Solomon said to you: you're laying the foundation for what it's going to take to save Aarde. Your sons all have a role to play; I don't know how but they do, and you need to let fate deal with them as it sees fit. Call for Oshún. Of your sons, he is the one the others look to for leadership. Explain to him the duties of his bloodline and what's expected of him."

"Of course, that's what you would say," Ozias spat. He stood from the table and pointed at Lyshyla. "For you, nothing matters but history and prophecy. Our lives don't matter. What we want doesn't matter! We're just pawns in your game of nations."

"Ozias..." Oadira began.

"No!" Ozias shouted. "I will say my peace! For 30 years we've been moved about from one calamity to the next, waiting and worrying, giving up what we want for the greater good. I was willing to choose that. My wife was willing to choose that, but I will not force it on my sons." He paced back and forth furiously, as if all his emotions were erupting at once. "Did you know that our sons have had chances to marry, but knew they would be called on to travel to Sahael and there was a possibility their wives would not be able to join them, so they fore bared? They sacrificed their happiness because of these callings, and now you're telling me they have to marry traitors for the greater good? No! I will not have it!"

Lyshyla stood, head bowed, and stepped toward the door. "I am sorry, Ozias," she said, voice quiet, tinged with emotion. "I understand your frustration. As Educators, we see the bigger picture, often forgetting the lives of the people around us. I know I have done this, and I apologize. That doesn't mean I am wrong though."

"Ozias and I need some time to think about this," Oadira said. "Give us some time, please, Lyshyla."

"Take all the time you need," Lyshyla said as she opened the door. "I'll return with Prince Oshún soon so the three of us can speak to him together." Lyshyla exited their personal quarters.

Once alone, Ozias sank back down in the chair beside the table. "What would she have us do? We've raised our children only to have to give them up to circumstance, chance, and fate because of the sins and recklessness of our lineage. So, it falls on them to clean up the sins and mistakes of the past?"

Oadira sat next to him and took his hand. "You're angry. You've been angry for a while."

"I have."

"Why?"

"Because of things like this. When you were performing the trails at Nereid's Monument, Lyshyla and I sat for months on the shores of the lake, waiting. And I realized, since we left Iceoth and said goodbye to my father, we've been waiting. I sent Osa, my best friend, to lead the people to Sahael to, what? Wait! Wait for us, wait for the right moment, the right bloodline, the right sunrise or whatever Lyshyla is going to tell us next. We wait and wait and wait, all so prophecies can be fulfilled, and other people can live their lives."

"I understand," Odira said, squeezing his hand. "When we met, we were so young; only two years older than Onika. We fell in love and ruled a kingdom. We fought in wars mere days after our sons were born. But I chose to fight in that war. I chose to love you, and the more I think about the circumstances of our lives, the more I understand how the choices I've made have allowed me to fulfil the words of Deities and prophets. I may wonder sometimes if I have any choices, and then I think of you. I didn't marry you and pretend to be someone else to trick your father because of some prophecy. I chose it. And I'd choose it again."

Ozias smiled and kissed her cheek. "So, what are you saying?"

"I'm saying we should let our sons choose. I don't like the situation, and if it were my choice I would charge out of here, but at the end of the day, it's not my choice. I've sacrificed, and so have you, but we chose that sacrifice. We shouldn't take that choice away from them. How does that make you feel?"

“The choice is theirs of course, but I don't want them to feel like that's the only choice.”

Oadira reached inside her traveling robes and pulled out Okavango's Heart on its golden chain around her neck. The sapphire stones glistened in the lamp light, accenting the nine different pieces being held together by their magnetic pull toward each other. It sat heavy in Oadira's palm, glowing slightly.

"This gem brought life back to Neir's Realm," Oadira said. "We will need it on our journey forward in ways we can't understand yet. We needed it to enter Timbuktu, and we'll need it to enter Sahael. I passed through trials to get it, and I would do it again. Yes, it was the only choice I could make if I wanted our people safe once more, but that doesn't mean I still didn't make the choice for myself."

Ozias smiled and nodded. He touched Okavango's Heart and his tattoos glowed for a moment.

"Oshún can take care of himself," Ozias admitted. "Lyshyla is right; he's become the leader of our boys. They'll follow him. Hell, everyone in Nieth City would have followed him. You've taught him everything he knows. If what Lyshyla says is true and they are a part of the first gathering, they'll need Oshún to lead them back to Sahael. How else could they do it? Only the ancient blood has access. At least with Oshún as the First Leader, it ensures that the Society of Secrets remains under Sahaelian control within each of the four kingdoms in Sahael." He touched Oadira's face. "You're right. I have been angry. Maybe it's time I let some of that go. You're also right about our sons making the choice themselves. We're all faced with choices that at the time don't seem to make sense. This is one of those choices that isn't about us. I don't understand how this helps Sahael, but Lyshyla would never tell us or you to do something that was wrong."

"You should tell her that," Oadira said. "You came at her pretty hard before she left."

"I guess I have a bit of resentment to work through. You have to admit, Educators certainly don't go out of their way to tell you what you need to know when you need to know it."

Oadira laughed. "Or maybe it's more accurate to say they only tell you something you need to know when you need to know it. They aren't going to volunteer information when it's not asked for, that's for sure."

A half hour later Lyshyla reentered their personal chambers with Prince Oshún.

“What are we going to do, Mother?” Oshún asked. "Oxum, Oya, Onika and I have been discussing our options, but we need yours and father's council."

“We have counsel, but no answers,” Oadira said. "What are your thoughts?"

"I don't know," Oshún shrugged. "We always knew taking wives in Nier's Realm would cause problems because of our bloodline and the trials we would likely need to pass through. Still, I never thought we'd have to marry anyone so much older than we are."

"They don't look old," Ozias said with a small smile. “They're royal blood, like all of us. You'd never know your mother and I were 50. All four of them are extremely good-looking girls."

“Is that so?” Oadira said, wondering how closely her husband had been looking.

"I didn't mean it like that," Ozias mumbled.

"Yes, they look young and beautiful," Oshún agreed. "But they must be close to 70 or 80 years old. I mean, they were adults at the time of the fall of Sahael if they helped Natas overthrow the royal bloodlines. Is that weird to have us marry women so much older?"

"You will live for many centuries, Oshún," Lyshyla replied. "After a thousand years, will a few decades truly matter? And beyond that, Educator Nortan made it clear that the four of them are of royal descent. Sy is of Orishan lineage, Ky is of Yoruban, Ny is of Hausan, and Fy is of Demirrian. This can’t be a coincidence that the blessings of Ibeji are with them,"

“He’s an Educator and knows more about our history and lineage than anyone other than Lyshyla,” Ozias said.

“Your eldest son, Oshún, is the one that has to bring them back into Sahael through marriage according to the Nairobi laws. Perhaps we can come up with an idea that still helps them get to Sahael safely.” Lyshyla explained.

“What are you suggesting?” Oadira asked.

“An agreement needs to be struck in which Oshún can be betrothed; they will not ask to marry any more of your sons. Educator Nortan is going to require all four leaders to be married to the eldest sons in each of the four bloodlines. Davú has been betrothed to Fy, the fourth leader of the Society of Secrets. That leaves Ny and Ky, who need to be betrothed to the princes of the Yoruban and Hausan bloodlines. As the leaders of the Chosen Bloodlines, you have the first rights on the oldest sons from each bloodline."

"So only Oshún would have to marry one of the bastard daughters?" Ozias asked.

“Who are we to subject one child to another, without the consent of their mother and father?” Oadira asked.

“The high queen and king of Sahael with the power to marry binding the bastard bloodlines back to Sahael. Oshún will need to be betrothed to the eldest of the leaders of the four bloodlines."

Oadira’s nose crinkled, unhappy with the supposed arrangement. “I didn’t know that. From what I can tell, it looks like she cannot wait to sink her claws into my son and turn him into something he’s not."

“That’s not true!" Lyshyla said with surprise passion. "The Society of Secrets are lost people without direction and guidance, in need of leadership. Oshún can provide them that direction and guidance, or they may be doomed to repeat the cycle once again as punishment. This is why Sahael was infiltrated and destroyed. It's also why Ishtar and Obatala imbued their bloodlines with special gifts and powers."

"What're you saying Lyshyla?" Oadira asked.

"The Society of Secrets are responsible for the role they played in Sahael's destruction. They used their gifts to supply Lord Commander Natas with all of the information he needed to invade Sahael. But before I called on Oshún, I spoke more with Educator Nortan again. He told me when Sahael fell from within, it was Sy, Ky, Ny, and Fy that saved you all from death at the hands of the Narsan. You wouldn't be here today if not for them. They regretted their actions almost immediately. They had no desire for anyone to die and tasted the ashes of their choice."

Oadira shook her head. "I need to hear this from them directly. I don't want to hear something like that secondhand. Go and bring her here so First Leader Sy, or whatever her title is, can tell me to my face."

Nodding, Lyshyla walked out and returned after a short time with First Leader Sy beside her. The woman glanced at Oshún, smiling slightly.

Oadira stood tall, looking down slightly on the woman. "Lyshyla tells me Educator Nortan claims you regretted your decision to betray Sahael, and you helped many escape. Is that true?"

"Yes," Sy explained. "But our actions still bring shame to us. Our Society single-handedly engineered the destruction and fall of western Aarde. We taught the Narsans our ways because Lord Commander Natas knew every weakness of every western nation. It's why the Narsan and Ennead were so effective and ruthless in their methods. They used phylacteries that contained White Darkness brought from the outer realms, darkness from the hosts that allowed Lord Commander Natas to control them. This made those who were consumed by the White Darkness in their governments make the decisions and pulling the strings from the beginning."

“What are these hosts?” Oadira asked.

“Yes, I would like to know as well,” Lyshyla stated.

Sy nodded. “There are many secrets hidden within western Aarde that will come to light in due time. But now is not the time. According to the Nairobi laws, the joining must be completed before our society gives all of itself to Sahael, Egyptus, and the Horn of Alkebulan. It’s imperative that we get to Sahael."

Oadira thought back to her flashback from when she was in the eddy before arriving in Synagogue. She had seen her mother and the fall of Sahael. Had she seen the vision to prepare her for this moment? To forgive the mistakes of the past and find a new way forward?

Touching her shoulder, Lyshyla seemed to understand Oadira's conflict. “Educator Nortan has made them aware of their past mistakes, getting them to make amends by saving you all, to ensure that a gathering would take place. This is why Lord Commander Natas sent the Narsans to kill all of them, forcing them into exile and closing themselves off from all of Aarde until the time was right."

“I understand,” Oadira said.

"I am sorry," Sy said, eyes suddenly wet. "My sisters are sorry. We felt betrayed, so we betrayed others. Even now we feel the regret. And I am sorry we so quickly threw the marriage proposal onto you and your sons. We have been dreaming of uniting our bloodlines for decades, and our arrival suddenly made that a possibility."

Lyshyla stepped between Sy and Oadira. “This betrothal

would be an agreement helping you get closer to Sahael where the marriage would take place after you've arrived; keep in mind the Chosen Right of Election will reside with Oshún, the first born of the triplets."

"The Orishan royal family will agree to these terms that you've outlined." Oadira said. "So long as Oshún chooses it to be so. Ozias and I will not make this choice for him."

Ozias turned to his son. "How do you feel about being betrothed to First Leader Sy? Is everything okay?"

Oshún rubbed his chin and gazed at the floor for some time.

"Well, Father," he answered eventually. "Sy is older than I am, but she is a rare beauty, wonderful, strong, and independent, much like you, Mother."

"You barely know the woman, Oshún," Oadira said. Yes, she wanted her son to make the choice, but now that he was talking and comparing Sy to her, Oadira didn't like where his choice might lead.

"How was it for you and Dad?" Oshún asked.

Oadira opened her mouth but then paused for a moment. She had no room to talk. She had to disguise herself as another woman to be married to Ozias. She didn't want to be a hypocrite.

"It's your choice, Oshún," Oadira said. "Just make sure you understand why you're making your choice."

"My intuition says First Leader Sy wants to love and be loved," Lyshyla said, nodding to Oshún. "But we know she has to remain strong for one-third of her people until she meets the right man. I feel Oshún is that man for her as I know she will be that woman for him."

"I'm in agreement, if this is what Oshún chooses," Ozias said, giving Oshún a thumbs up.

Oshún looked at Sy. "I will do this for my people. My parents have taught me the nobility of sacrifice as they have served the greater good my entire life. So long as we take time to get to know each other better and strive for the type of love my mother and father enjoy, then I will be betrothed to you, First Leader Sy."

A smile brightened Sy's face.

"It's settled then," Lyshyla clapped. "Oshún and Sy are to be betrothed and married in Sahael once Oshún leads them there. You'll also need to make the decision for the other three bloodlines, for the firstborn of each. Queen Oadira, you should inform Educator Nortan that Oshún has agreed. It's important that it comes out of your mouth."

"Yes," Oadira said. "I will."

"Repeat after me, so Oshún can hear it and repeat after you," Lyshyla said.

"Repeat what? What is it I'm repeating?" Oadira asked.

"The Oath of Promise," Lyshyla said. "Such is the custom of this people, as it has always been since my days in Timbuktu. Repeat after me: 'I promise to do my best to understand and respect my personal responsibilities, to First Leader Sy as prime first leader. I promise to marry Sy, when we return to Sahael.'"

Oadira and Oshún repeated the exact same words. For Oadira, the line about personal responsibility to First Leader Sy made her uncomfortable for her son, but she knew this was now Oshún's choice, and she would respect it.

"Doesn't Sy need to repeat something for Oshún?" Oadira asked. "It's only fair."

"No," Lyshyla answered. "Sy will cite the Oath of Promise with Educator Nortan; afterward, you'll have to stay here and live among the Society of Secrets until you return to Sahael."

“I’m still having a hard time with this, but I’ll be patient for now,” Oadira said.

Over the next few days, the family explored the area, getting to know Synagogue and its people. Much like Oadira thought upon their arrival, they were a proud people who had been humbled. They still walked with haughty superiority, but their circumstances in the damaged city acted as a balance against their pride.

After a week, Oadira and Ozias were summoned to the north end of Synagogue where Lyshyla met them on a path leading into a carved entryway of solid stone in the side of a snowcapped mountain. The granite had been opened with masterful skill, leaving behind smooth surfaces that reminded Oadira of the plaza walls in Nieth City.

"Educator Nortan wants to see both of you," Lyshyla told them as they walked into the mountain. Cold air blew into Oadira's face, blowing her long braids.

"What does he want to talk about?" Ozias asked. "He already has one of our sons betrothed to Sy. What more can he want?"

"I think he wants to teach," Lyshyla replied.

"He wouldn't be an educator if he didn’t," Oadira said, shaking her head.

The opening in the mountain led to a long passageway with ornate carvings on the walls. Eventually it opened on a cavernous room with arched ceilings and pillars carved from the granite itself. In the center of the space stood Educator Nortan. Surrounding him was a fully intact Nairohenge Gate.

“You have a Nairohenge Gate here?” Oadira asked in surprise. The tall rectangular stones stood in a circular pattern just as she had seen in Timbuktu.

“After the fall of Sahael," Educator Nortan began, "the Nairohenge gates across Aarde retracted into the ground, including these. They reemerged, however, one week ago after your arrival through the eddy. Lord Commander Natas thought that all of them were destroyed, not knowing that they retracted into the ground, preventing him from having access to them. Due to the shifting of the lands, this revealed a crevice and the Nairohenge Gate’s inside of it. We cannot use them to get you to Sahael, but as promised, with your son's betrothal to Lady Sy, we have ways of getting you access to the forbidden lands. The Scions will escort you all to the edge of the river; there you will see a large eddy that will take you through the Nazaum channel. From there, you need to catch the current that will take you to the shores of western Nazaum. that is your next destination."

"Thank you, Educator Nortan," Lyshyla said with a bow. "We will set out at first light tomorrow. Sahael will be reclaimed.”

Educator Nortan raised his hand as if to stop further discussion. “One more thing. I spoke with Oshún several days ago regarding the Promise of Betrothal.” Nortan looked at Oshún. “Have you told them about it?”

Oshún looked down quickly and then up at his mother and father. “I wasn’t sure how to.”

“What is the Promise of Betrothal?” Ozias asked.

“It is that the betrothed are to be together, unseparated, until their marriage,” Nortan informed. “Isn’t this right, Educator Lyshyla?”

“Yes,” Lyshyla answered quietly.

“Wait, that means…” Oadira began.

“It means that I am waiving the Promise of Betrothal for eighty days,” Educator Nortan said. “It took eighty days for Ishtar to reach Obatala after the first sunrise, and thus Oshún will have the same eighty days to return to his betrothed. Oshún has agreed that at the end of that time frame he is to return to Sanctuary and his future bride."

Oadira glared at Oshún. How dare he make a commitment like that without talking to her and Ozias first? They needed him, his strength and leadership.

"I agreed," Oshún said, placing his hand on Oadira's shoulder. "It is what you or Father would have done. I did it for Sahael and all people."

"And how do you expect to get back here, Son?" Oadira asked. "We have no idea how far we're going to have to go. Eighty days is nothing!"

"I have faith, Mother," Oshún smiled. "You taught me to fight and to conquer. But you also taught me faith, especially over the last year. I have faith a way will be provided, and I will return here safely. Trust in that."

"Are you sure, Oshún?" Ozias asked.

"I am, Father."

"Eighty days," Nortan said, arms wide. "No more. Now, are you ready to set out?"

"We are," Lyshyla replied before Oadira could make any kind of protest.

"So it is written," Nortan replied. "But a word of caution: when you arrive, be on your guard. Everything in Nazaum, from the plants to the animal life, will be larger than anything you've ever seen. Be prepared to face death like you never have before."

CHAPTER II

THE UNTAMED LANDS OF NAZAUM

The other side of Aarde, Western Nazaum

The royal family left the following morning, with Lyshyla by their side as always. They traveled through Nazaum's channel, following the currents beneath the water's surface and arriving in the unknown lands of Nazaum three days later. Covered in sand, gray mountains, and Marula Trees, Nazaum consisted of jagged rocks sharp as blades, making it difficult to enter the land from the outside.

As they all washed up on the coast, Oadira touched the warm sand and gazed at the rocky formations beyond that looked like thousands of knife points as tall as an elephant.

"That was a wild ride! I have never seen water move so fast! Where are we?" Oxum yelled in excitement.

"The shores of Nazaum," Oadira answered. "Finding cover needs to be our main concern before the sandworms eat us."

"Sandworms! What are sandworms?" Oxum asked.

"Sandworms are large, twelve-foot-long, circular creatures

that dig deep beneath the sand, creating traps in quicksand," Oya replied like a professor annoyed at a student for neglecting their studies. "You guys always made fun of me for studying insects and animal life. It will pay off today. Sandworms kill you by suffocation and then consume you with their large mouths, eating you with a single swallow and using acid to break you down as you dissolve in their stomach. They aren't the only dangerous monsters we need to be aware of here."

"What types of monsters are there that we need to be worried about?" Onika asked as they started walking across the beach toward the outcroppings of stone.

Oya stretched his neck to the right. "Monsters such as trapdoor spiders, wolf spiders, scorpions, and centipedes. We need to avoid all of them. They are larger than normal here on Nazaum, especially the insects, the Marula Trees, and the rocks. The sunlight will fade quickly, and when it's completely dark, we'll have to find a place high in the Marula Trees for shelter."

"For what reasons?" Oshún asked.

"To avoid the mashers," Oya said. "You know, if you spent half as much time studying insects as you did flirting with the girls of Neir's Realm when we were teenagers, you would know what to do if you stepped on a masher."

The group weaved through a maze of sharp stone that seemed to go on forever. Within a few minutes it became difficult to tell which direction they were going.

"It's going to get dark soon," Lyshyla warned as several oversized dragonflies buzzed overhead. "Finding higher ground is a must if we want to avoid the mashers."

"Okay, I know you're just trying to scare us," Oshún said. "But what are these mashers?"

"I bet you wish you'd studied instead of flirted," Oya

chuckled.

Oshún punched his brother in the shoulder playfully. "Shut up!"

“Mashers are these large bugs that have an outer gray shell that forms into a circular, indestructible ball," Lyshyla answered as the two brothers began hitting each other in a mock battle. "They roll around throughout the forest, smashing everything in their path. They use the trees as a means to mow down, slow down, and trap animals to smash them. Then they come out of their shell to eat what they have killed and retreat back into their indestructible shells and do it again."

“This place is crazy!” yelled Oxum.

Lyshyla jumped up on a boulder and looked ahead of them. “This is Nazaum, a large, sandy, mountainous mass of untamed land, encircled by mountains everywhere you go. The only way to get inside is to climb up and over it or to go through the mountains if we can’t find a port opening."

The seven-member group soon found a port opening through the maze of sharp rocks. They looked down on a sandy expanse with large boulders sticking out from the dunes.

"Stay on top of large rocks to avoid the quicksand and the sandworms," Oya ordered as he and Lyshyla leaped to the nearest boulder. "They can feel our vibrations, so don't touch the sand."

As they leaped from rock to rock, Oadira noticed trees growing from the sand, and small patches of forest. Small lakes dotted the landscape teeming with foot-long cockroaches and centipedes longer than Oadira's arm. The plants and average insects were all larger than normal compared to the other side of Aarde.

"I've heard you can roast those giant roaches over a fire, and they are quite delicious," Oya said as several bugs climbed up the rocks next to them as they passed. "We should try it tonight once we find shelter."

"Will you shut up about eating bugs and stuff?" Onika said as he dodged a massive centipede scurrying by his foot.

“Looking for shelter should be on everyone’s mind," Lyshyla said. She stopped on one of the rocks and pointed to a larger boulder in the distance. "We should make our way there, to that boulder and the small forest beyond. We may find some shelter there. We can’t sleep out in the open."

"I don't want to know why," Ozias said.

"At night," Oya began in a menacing voice, "the centipedes come up from below the ground and carry you away in your sleep. You don’t realize you’re in their lair until it's too late. They start squeezing you, breaking every bone in your body, turning you into mush with their razor-sharp legs, and then drinking you like liquid."

"Shut up, Oya!" Oxum shouted. "This isn't funny."

"It is for me," Oya chuckled.

Oadira’s eyes widened as she looked out over the forest before her. The Marula Trees had grown to at least twice the size she had ever seen. Instead of reaching 20 to 40 feet in the air and that same distance in diameter, they were commonly 80 feet tall, with thick, knotted trunks.

“What are those?” Onika asked, pointing to the high branches overhead.

Several wooden structures hung from the massive limbs like dangling huts of twig, moss, and thatch.

“They look like giant bird nests almost,” whispered Oxum. “Are there giant birds here?”

“Are they going to eat us?” Onika asked, wiping sweat

from his brow.

"The Wiru built these treehouses," Lyshyla answered. "They are for people, not birds."

"It must have taken a lot of time to build these," Oadira said.

"How is it that you know of these places?" Ozias asked as he gazed at the structures above.

Before Lyshyla could answer, the group was startled by a man with a walking stick who stepped out from behind the large tree in front of them.

"Welcome," said the man with a smile. He stood six-feet-eight-inches tall, with a white beard and dreadlocked hair. Despite his age, he possessed a long, slender build with well-defined muscles. "This treehouse has been my post for a long time."

"What is your name?" Ozias asked.

"I am Ztaum," he answered. "You are welcome here. The floor of the forest and sands beyond are not safe, particularly after nightfall, which is fast approaching."

"Thank you for allowing us to be here. But why are you here by yourself?" Lyshyla asked.

"My stepfather and the Wiru people made a promise, allowing me refuge in one of their treehouses so long as I would do the same for others wandering these lands. My treehouses were constructed to protect people from the dangerous grounds—the pumas, gorillas, and crocodiles and many more beasts."

"Great," Oshún said, shaking his head. "And I thought the centipedes sounded bad. Now we have to worry about gorillas and crocodiles too?"

"I hate this place," Onika lamented.

Ztaum stepped closer to Oadira, mouth slightly agape.

"Your eyes . . . Are . . . are you the family of royalty looking to return back to Sahael?"

"Yes," Oadira said with a proud smile. Finally, they met someone in this land that seemed happy to see them.

Oxum looked around, eyes suddenly wide. "Hey! I read about this place when we were in Timbuktu."

"When?" Oya asked, an incredulous tinge to his voice. "I never saw you reading with me in the archives."

"I read about it in the royal library," Oxum said.

"Sure, you did," Oya replied.

"I did!" shouted Oxum.

"Uh-huh! Whatever you say, Oxum," said Oya.

"But I really did! You don't know! You weren't there!" Oxum's voice got bolder as he shouted.

"Knock it off, both of you," Oadira interrupted. "You sound like bickering teenagers. You're adults. Act like it, or I'll knock both of you upside the head like that time in the tunnels when you awakened the Treep Spiders."

"Yes, Mother," both men said as if transported to their childhood once again.

Lyshyla approached Ztaum. "You're not of the Wiru, and you certainly don't share their vast size at all."

"I've been waiting for your arrival for some time. My stepfather and I take turns with shifts," Ztaum answered. "But please, before we continue, let us ascend to safety in one of the treehouses. The sun is on the verge of setting, and it is always best to seek shelter early. You will find they are quite comfortable inside.

Oadira climbed behind Ztaum, leading the family into the

boughs high above. As promised, the treehouse was quite spacious, with cot-like beds hanging along the walls. A stone pit in the center held smoldering coals, while an opening in the top allowed any smoke from a larger blaze to billow out. In one corner of the rounded space hung a large net that seemed to writhe as if alive.

"Are those…?" Oxum whispered to Oya.

"I have captured enough roaches for several days," Ztaum said, hitting the net with his walking stick. "There should be enough for all of us tonight. I can scavenge more in the morning. That is one good thing about the Nazaum: finding food is easy."

"And swallowing it without throwing up is probably harder," Oxum chuckled.

After stoking the fire and roasting several massive cockroaches, The group ate in relative silence. While Oya seemed to enjoy the meal immensely, Oadira found chewing on insect legs difficult despite the flavor being somewhat pleasant.

"My people are in need of your assistance," Ztaum said once the meal had ended. "We are being hunted and are on the verge of being wiped out for no reason other than the fact that we exist."

"Why is it that you are all being hunted?" Ozias asked as he took a bite of what remained of his roasted roach.

"The Wiru made a pact with the forest people of Nade four hundred years ago to provide them with protection. That pact disrupted the balance, tilting the balance of power on this land. The Wiru started hunting the people of Nade in this forest. Out of respect for the Narsans, the Wiru broke their sacred pact with the Nazaummians, which signaled their own destruction."

"What do you mean by their destruction?" Oxum asked, rubbing his head.

"The Wiru entered the conflict that put the Nazaummians

against them," Ztaum said.

"What is so special about your people?" Oxum asked.

"I'm not sure how to answer your question, but your arrival has something to do with it."

"How so?" Oxum asked.

Ztaum stood and brought them hot soup from the fire to wash down their roaches. "The fact that your family is finally here is all that matters. We'll travel at first light after you all have rested."

"Can you finish explaining about the conflict your people were involved in?" Oadira asked. "So, what happened next?"

"During the fighting and perpetual war, our enemies united the untamed lands of Nazaum and now fight against the Wiru and my people," Ztaum explained.

"What did they do next?" Oadira asked.

"We made preparations and then disappeared inside of the sanctuary, hidden away from the inhabitants of Nazaum."

"So where did they go?" Oxum asked.

"I don't know if anyone truly knows," Ztaum shook his head. "They disappeared with the forest people for unexplainable reasons, unknown to me and the Wiru people. However, with that said, it doesn't matter at this moment. My focus is helping you and your family get to Sahael, so we'll have to travel through this land to get there. I'll take first watch."

Ztaum rose and stood by the entrance of the treehouse as the others got comfortable in their hammocks.

As the morning approached, Oadira woke to the sounds of thousands of birds flying through the forest. Their melodic sounds reminded her of music from the most beautiful voices. She stepped from her hammock and walked to the doorway to observe the birds as the colorful fowl flocked in swirling eddies of life. As they dove in the distance, Oadira noticed something up against the mountains that started emanating a pale-yellow light. She rubbed her eyes, yawned, and squinted, but she couldn't make out what she was seeing.

"What are you looking at?" Ozias asked as he approached her from behind, wooden floor creaking beneath his feet.

"There's something that looks like an opening into the mountain on the ground," Oadira said. "There is a light or something coming from it."

"An opening?" Ozias asked.

"I'm not entirely sure. I'm going to travel down below to get a better look," Oadira suggested.

"I'm coming with you," Ozias said. "Let's wake the boys and Lyshyla."

As the family prepared to leave the treehouse, Ztaum climbed up the ladder carrying a net filled with what looked like oversized grubs or maggots. The six-inch long worms writhed against each other.

"Are you leaving so soon?" the old man asked as he threw the net onto the floor of the treehouse. "You haven't had breakfast yet, and you'll need your strength."

Oya grabbed one of the grubs excitedly. "Do we eat them raw, or cook them first?"

"They're best raw," Ztaum grinned.

Avoiding looking at the worms wiggling at her feet, Oadira pointed toward the mountain. "Ztaum, what is that dark spot on the hills to the west? It looks like it's glowing."

"I don't know, to be honest," he admitted. "I know nothing or old relics or histories beyond my own people and the promises of Sahael. It is a series of circular stones taller than a man. At times the symbols will glow on their sides, but I don't know what they mean."

Oadira looked at Lyshyla, whose face seemed suddenly excited. "It could be a Nairo Gate?"

"Very possibly," Lyshyla smiled. "We should go…" she looked down at the grubs, "…before breakfast."

Everyone in Aum's treehouse descended down the vines to the ground. Following Ztaum, they wandered hidden paths, sometimes walking on large, entangled tree trunks, sometimes on the ground itself, but always heading more or less toward the west…towards Sahael, lost somewhere over the horizon.

"You'll need to hurry," Ztaum warned. "The Mashers will be coming for us. they can feel the vibrations of our feet. The west is their domain, so the closer we draw to the mountain, the more likely they are to feel our presence."

After several hours of walking, Oadira began to wish she had eaten one of the grubs. Her stomach growled and she was reminded of her diminished powers here in the realm. Eventually they stepped from the jungle and looked out on a cliff face of gray rock. Less than a quarter mile away she could see the crevice with its pale-yellow glow.

"What do you see?" Ozias asked, stepping next to Oadira.

"I don't know what I'm seeing. We'll have to get closer," Oadira said.

Ztaum led them to the crevice, a large gash in the

mountainside at least 300 feet tall and at least that wide at the base. Once inside, Oadira could make out tall rectangular stones with glowing symbols just like the Nairohenge Gates she had seen in Nier's Realm and Synagogue City.

"It's a single Nairo gate blending in with the mountain," Lyshyla breathed. "They were deactivated when Sahael fell. There are several of these types of gates that seal everything off from the outside from getting inside. The symbols lead into the crevice of the mountain where the opening ends, with Orishan symbols along the walls of the crevice and three other sets of symbols from the four different lineages."

Oxum examined the rock structures with their pale sun-kissed glow. He ran his hands across the smooth surface. His eyes suddenly turned cerulean. The yellow light of the symbols slowly shifted to blue as well.

"Look!" Oxum shouted as he pointed at the symbols. "What's happening?"

"The gate is opening!" Lyshyla said.

Lightning shot from the center of the circled stones as a stiff wind filled the dark cavern. Thunder rumbled in their ears.

"If the mashers didn't know we were here before, they do now," Onika shouted over the gale.

With a blast of blue energy, a portal opened before them. Swirling shades of blue and purple mixed like water flowing down a drain.

"How did it open without Navigators?" Ozias asked as his cloak pulled toward the portal.

"It's not a standard gate," Lyshyla yelled. "It's a local doorway that will take us somewhere within a few miles of where we are now. I haven't seen one in many decades."

Ztaum suddenly cried out. "Everyone, hurry up and enter! The mashers are coming this way!"

Several large gray balls rolled quickly toward the crevice entrance, smashing into trees and crushing everything in their path. One unrolled from their protective shell into a ten-foot-tall insect with a dozen legs and razor sharp pinchers and teeth.

"Mashers!" Oshún cried, pointing at the encroaching creatures.

"Hurry," Lyshyla urged. "Into the portal. The unknown is better than the known at this point!"

They hurried through the portal one by one. Oadira and Ozias passed through last, feeling the tingling and pull of the gateway as they were transported somewhere else entirely.

Oadira's eyes blinked as sunlight replaced the darkness of the cave. She felt grass between her toes where seconds before had been only bare rock. Pollen tickled her nose from flowers in full bloom. They stood in a lush valley surrounded by towering mountains topped with snow. The valley was small, but fertile, with waterfalls cascading in the distance. Marula Trees grew everywhere. The air was clear and pure, easy to breathe, as if it rejuvenated the lungs with every breath. Animals, birds, and fish filled the area and the stream beside them. Children ran around laughing in a clearing to their left.

"What is this place?" Ozias asked.

"You have arrived and entered this sanctuary through the Wiru Gate," a deep, gravelly voice boomed behind them. They turned to see a heavy set, muscular man, wide bodied, and significantly bigger than King Ozias and his family. He stood ten-feet tall, skin dark, a large afro covering his massive head.

"Who are you?" Oadira asked.

"I am Aum," the man answered with a smile. "The gate has

led you directly into Wirusa's Sanctuary. It has been many years since the gate has been activated. It has remained dormant, waiting for one of the Chosen Bloodline to pass through. What brings you here?"

"We seek passage through your lands to get to Sahael," Oadira answered.

Aum clapped his hands and grinned broadly. "My people have been waiting for your arrival the moment you entered the forest on the other side of this mountain yesterday."

"How is that possible?" Oadira asked.

"The Marula Trees talk and communicate with the roots, leaves, and branches, alerting me of your arrival. The Signs of the Times are upon Aarde."

"Why are you all alone hidden in your own lands?" Lyshyla asked. "How far are we from the local gateway we found in the crevice?"

"Only a few miles," Aum replied. "The gate is beyond the peak here to our west. And as to why we are here…my people are being hunted. It is to prevent their eradication. We've been forced to hide and preserve ourselves inside of Wirusa's Sanctuary. This sanctuary was found by chance by me, and it has aided my people in escaping the persecution of the Narsans and to preserve our way of life from extermination. I had to wait to engage you all until you had made it through the mountain crevice. I recognized your eyes and tattoos as they lit up in magnificence. Please follow me. Time is of the essence."

"Where are you taking us?" Lyshyla asked.

"You'll find out in due time," Aum said.

They walked for about fifteen minutes through the sanctuary, observing all the wildlife of Aarde. Large insects, lady bugs, mosquitoes, and frogs darted here and there, all oversized and robust. Mouse-sized wasps with giant nests the size of houses hung from the large Marula Trees. Children waved at the group as they passed, several of them as tall as 16-year-old Onika.

"What is this place?" asked Oadira as a butterfly the size of an eagle cast a shadow on her. "How is everything so big, including some of the children here?"

"You're in the kingdom of Wirusa," Aum answered. "It is a kingdom made out of trees, stones, and mountains that are beautiful. Wirusa is where all of the giants in Aarde live. It extends from the ground to the trees, circling the whole perimeter as it rains continually. To preserve my people, the Wiru welcome everyone with open arms, thanks to my daughter, Uzuri, who saved a Wirusa child from death at the hands of the Narsans. They had gained control of the Nazaummian, my former people. As you can see, there is a mix of giants, half-giants, and Wiru people of average height. I was actually exiled from my tribe because I married a Wiru woman. I was later forgiven because of my daughter's bravery. Ah, and I see her approaching now!"

As Aum spoke, Uzuri made her presence known, walking through the forest with her security detail; large Wiru giants circled her for her protection. Uzuri stood six-feet-five-inches tall. She possessed brownish-blue eyes that captivated Oadira. The woman had short hair that was beautiful, with white, ivory teeth, and unblemished chestnut skin. She spoke quietly to her security detail as she pointed to different areas of the forest. It was clear she was busy.

"My daughter is in charge of the restoration projects here in the sanctuary," Aum continued as they walked past Uzuri and her giant guards. "Many species in the forest beyond the mountains are threatened because of war and thoughtlessness. We preserve them here so that when Sahael reigns once more, we may transplant them to their homelands."

Through the trees ahead, Oadira saw a massive palace structure made of white stones in a simple rectangular design. It stood 100 feet high and glistened in the late morning sun.

"This is Wir Palace," Aum said.

Uzuri quickly left her Wirusan guards, entering Wir Palace as she departed. Oxum could not keep his eyes off her.

"You were looking at the half-giant pretty closely," Oya said, nudging his brother.

"I just…" Oxum stumbled. "Wanted to…see…shut up."

Before entering the palace, Aum stopped and sent his guards inside to speak with Lyshyla and the royal princes. Oadira and Ozias stood with him on the palace steps alone.

"I know that the two of you are looking for a way into Sahael," Aum said as he folded his arms. "I will help you in any way I can.

"Why are you helping us?" Oadira asked. "You're safe here in the mountains. No one can find you."

"Solomon is the reason I'm helping," Aum said. Oadira hadn't heard Solomon's name in quite some time. She had only met him on three separate occasions over 30 years ago, but he had put her on this path to reclaiming her homeland. If he was involved with this hidden garden, she would trust the people and their aid.

"He made us promise that if we crossed paths, my people were to help you find a way to help save the Wiru people," Aum continued. "It would be left up to those I help if they would grant a favor in return to a dying man. Follow me into the palace. In time, I'll take you to the giant city of Wirusa and the great palace of Wirusa."

As they entered the palace of Wir, Aum introduced his daughter, Uzuri. She bowed and pointed out the beautifully handcrafted walls made of wood and the carvings telling the story of their people. Everything from the tables, doors, chairs, and even the throne room itself were all made out of the most exquisite wood.

"While the exterior of the palace is pale limestone," Uzuri said in a pleasant voice, "The interior is all wood, as to respect Aarde and all life that grows there. We are masters of woodcraft."

They were greeted by Wirusa guards standing in the royal halls among wooden, floor-to-ceiling pillars. They made their way into the throne room, where Lyshyla, Oshún, Oxum, Oya, and Onika already waited. As Aum took his rightful place on the Wirwood throne, Uzuri followed him and sat right beside her father.

Uzuri continued to spark a physical attraction that stunned anyone who came into contact with her beauty and elegance. Her body, hair, face, and skin were perfect beyond all description. Oadira had never seen anyone with such natural grace and presence.

"Wow! She's gorgeous!" remarked Oxum, who caught everyone's attention with his bold statement.

Uzuri lowered her head into her arms, trying not to laugh and blush.

"We apologize for our son's…inappropriate outburst," Ozias said with a cough.

Aum smiled. "Don't worry. I am used to my daughter garnering the attention of strapping men. She has a powerful effect on most people. It is a blessing and a curse. And from the color of her cheeks, I feel she is flattered by the comment. I sense you are all hungry. After a meal, I will have Uzuri lead you through the village here in our sanctuary lands."

"Can I be your escort as you show me around the city?"

Oxum asked, stepping closer to Uzuri.

"I think that's a wonderful idea," Ruler Aum said.

"Of course," Uzuri replied.

Servants brought in platters of greens and steaming meats. Everything smelled good, but Oadira wondered whether the meat was insect in nature or something else. She felt it better to remain in ignorance as she consumed the meal with gratitude.

Once the plates had been taken away, Uzuri stood from her seat and laced her arm through Oxum's. "Do you still wish to escort me as I give you a tour?"

"I do!" Oxum beamed.

"After that," Aum said, wiping his mouth with a cloth napkin, "I urge you all to rest and relax. To reach the gates that will lead you to Sahael you must first reach the great Wiruan City, which is a seven-day trek. We leave at the beginning of the week's first light, in three days' time, if you still wish to make the journey."

"We do," Oadira nodded.

The boys followed Uzuri out of the throne room while Oadira, Ozias, and Lyshyla remained behind.

"Where is your wife?" Ozias asked. "I was surprised when your daughter sat with you on the throne."

Aum gave a soft chuckle and looked to the ground with a smile. The smile faded quickly, leaving behind an empty stare. "She died giving birth to Uzuri."

"I apologize, I meant no offense," Ozias said.

"It's okay. You didn't know. The first time we met was when she got lost in the forest. When I found her, she had been severely wounded. I cared for her and nursed her back to health. Throughout our time together, we fell in love as she was accepted among my people as we were married. She was small compared to the people of my tribe. She became the queen of our citizens." A frown pulled down Aum's cheeks. "On her deathbed, she admitted to me that she was wounded by a group of Narsan and Ennead soldiers and left for dead. Thankfully, with the help of the forest, she was hidden from a man in black. She told me the man in black looked for her day and night, wanting to kill her. During her flight, she found the Wiru crevice. The crevice is also where we both met Solomon and promised to wait for your arrival as part of the agreement for revealing the crevice to us."

The man in black.

Oadira had seen him herself, in the forests of Iceoth just before the birth of her triplets. It was believed he was the son of Natas himself, Damien. He had been sent by his father to search Aarde for the four missing princesses, Oadira and her cousins. He wore a cloak so dark no light could escape it. She had seen his eyes that night in the forest, orange against his dark skin.

"What happened to your wife's people?" Lyshyla asked, returning Oadira to the conversation.

"They were wiped out. Uzuri is the last of her bloodline," Aum said.

"I understand. I am sorry for your loss." Oadira fondly placed her hand on Aum's and gave a gentle smile. They had all suffered because of Natas and the witans who succumbed to their own racist ideals. No one from their ethnic group was immune, whether giant or otherwise.

Aum clapped his hands and stood. "Why don't we catch up with Uzuri and your sons so you can learn more about this land. You three run ahead. I'll catch up in a few moments."

Oadira nodded and she, Ozias and Lyshyla followed Aum outside. The afternoon air was warm and pleasant. Standing across from a grouping of trees stood Oadira's sons, with the beautiful Uzuri. Oxum and Uzuri walked around under guard as she pointed to finely crafted wooden buildings in the village across the grassy clearing.

"As you can see," Uzuri said, "most of our buildings are made of the finest and hardest wood from the local trees. We only harvest trees that are aged and dying, so the young branches can continue to flourish. The older the tree, the harder the wood becomes. Many of our weapons are also made from wood, since the material is so strong here in Nazaum."

"I have noticed that this place is surrounded entirely by mountains," Oxum asked Uzuri as Oadira and her husband approached. "So, you look different physically compared to the Wiru people here. There has to be a story there."

"It's been some time since I've really taken note of the landscape," Uzuri said as she looked around. "Many years ago, my great-grandfather, Waqar, united the four Wirusan tribes, working day and night to create this sanctuary. They moved mountains to construct this place with Solomon's help using the Ankh emblems made of emerald, hematite, sapphire, and turquoise stones. Their emblems gave the people impossible strength. They made the mountains unclimbable for anyone who attempted to travel to the kingdom of Wirusa."

"I understand," replied Oxum. "So, your father is King Waqar's last remaining heir?"

"After Solomon spoke with Aum's father, he said that place would house his bloodline one day and that his daughter would marry a prince of royal blood from an Ancient and Chosen Bloodline," Uzuri explained.

"A born son of the Orishan bloodline?" Oxum asked.

Before she could say anything else, Oadira stepped

forward, scowling.

"We're getting ahead of ourselves, Oxum," she said. "And you are being impolite to the point of rudeness."

Oxum dropped his head, dreadlocks falling over his shoulders. "I am sorry, Mother. I meant no disrespect to our hostess."

"It's fine," Uzuri grinned. "And to answer your question, yes, I was told that one day I would fall in love to save the Wiru people." She suddenly looked down at the grass, face sad. "I must because…my father is dying. Solomon instructed my father to wait for the Signs of the Times to reach the sanctuary."

Aum is dying? Oadira thought. *He seems so strong and vital. What could he be dying from?*

"I see your father approaching," Oxum said, suddenly dropping Uzuri's arm. The towering king stepped close to them and bowed.

"It's time to come inside," Aum said, motioning back toward the palace. "There are preparations to be made if we are to have the supplies to travel west. We're not going to have the opportunity to stop and rest; this trek will test your mental fortitude and patience."

Aum looked at his daughter and then at Oxum.

"I can see that the two of you are captivated by each other, and that is okay, but for right now, I want you both to be where you can be seen for your own safety. As for the rest of you, relax in the warm afternoon for a time. I had hoped we could continue our discussion, but it will unfortunately have to wait."

Aum walked away with Uzuri, but Lyshyla stepped forward. "There are matters we need to discuss," she said. "We only have seventy-six days until one of the royal family must return to Sanctuary. Our time is short."

"When we arrive in the capital city, we'll discuss what needs to be done," Aum said. His eyes looked suddenly weary as he turned back toward the palace and continued walking.

CHAPTER III

THE WIRUSA OF NAZAUM

Nazaum, Wirusa Sanctuary

As promised, on the third day, at the rising of the sun that began the week, Oadira set off with her family toward the east, led by Aum, Uzuri, and a group of their strongest guards, all of which towered over even Ozias.

After several full days of traveling over the mountains and down into jungled valleys, the legs of the royal family grew tired. Seeing this and not wanting their travel time to be slowed, Aum ordered to have the royal family and his daughter ride large tortoises for the remaining days. The tortoises moved efficiently through the forest day and night, allowing the royal family the ability to sleep and eat as they continued to travel, staying on their schedule. Giraffes, gazelles, and silverback gorillas all wandered along their path during the seven-day journey. Each passing morning, Aum seemed to grow weaker and less talkative. Uzuri would often have him ride her turtle while she walked in his stead.

The tortoises themselves amazed Oadira. They were as big as horses and surprisingly consistent in their speed. After the guards had corralled the creatures, they had quickly crafted makeshift saddles from vines and pieces of wood lying on the forest floor. These people truly were impressive craftsmen. The turtles could even swim, providing the traveling party with the ability to cross Naum Lake quickly while the guards swam around them.

As they waded through the water on the backs of the tortoise, Oadira heard a strange buzzing sound above her. Looking around, she recognized large mosquitos with knife-like pointers barreling down at her and the group.

"Evade! Evade!" one of the guards yelled as he pulled out a shield and swam in front of Princess Uzuri.

"It's a swarm!" Aum shouted.

The insects descended in a thick cloud, each with a six-inch long proboscis ready to strike.

"Use your artes as best you can!" Ozias ordered.

As if in response, Onika blinked his eyes twice, making them light up cerulean, and enabling him to use his Orishan gifts. Onika's tattoos lit up, allowing him to conjure needle shuriken and firing them at the large mosquitos. Oadira did the same, but the effort was far more difficult than it had ever been before. She couldn't wait to leave Nazaum and western Aarde so her full abilities could return. Using a small ethereal blade, she cut two of the mosquitos in half, but there were too many.

"Dive into the water!" Aum ordered.

Cold water surrounded Oadira as she plunged gratefully into her element. Even so, the mosquitos continued stabbing at the group repeatedly. Oadira realized she had other tools at her disposal though. She opened her mind and communicated with the flying fish in the waters below. As if responding to a command, large fish appeared from out of the lake and began to eat the mosquitos until the swarm buzzed away.

Splashing onto the shore, Oadira assessed the damage to their party. Unfortunately, the attack left the group with multiple mosquito bites that swelled up with oozing pus.

All except her and her sons.

"How were those mosquitos able to puncture everyone else's skin and not ours?" Onika asked as he rubbed a spot on his arm where a mosquito had tried to sting him.

Oadira nodded, realizing that, while weakened, some of their latent abilities remained strong. "When you blink your eyes twice," she told her son, "the Orishan cerulean within your eyes lights up, encrusting your body to make you indestructible. If you don't activate the Orishan cerulean within your eyes and if you're wounded and blink your eyes, the aura can heal you completely. You can see that myself, you and your brothers all did this instinctively. Your father did not."

Ozias cursed as he scratched at a large swelling bump on his chest and two others on his arms. Lyshyla was in a similar predicament, as were Aum and his entourage. Uzuri on the other hand seemed to be completely unharmed, as if her beauty even affected the mosquitos and they had avoided harming her because of it.

The shores of the east end of the lake were littered with dead animals swollen from the mosquitoes.

"How is this lake filled with so much death?" Lyshyla asked.

"This is new and unheard of," Aum said as he kicked over an oversized rodent rotting in the sun. "There is something happening in the sanctuary. Even the water has changed. It seems to have reacted to your presence, Oadira. We must travel warily. Even so, we should arrive at our destination by nightfall."

After several hours, they finally crested a rocky ridge and looked down on a city that filled an entire valley. Spires reached to the sky, and each building seemed bigger than anything Oadira had ever seen, even in the sanctuary. People filled the streets, and even from their perch on the ridge high above, Oadira could tell they were all giants like King Aum.

"Welcome to Wiruan!" Aum said to everyone as they started down the path toward the metropolis.

"We've arrived. Please follow me," Aum said. They followed Aum through the city as they were greeted by the Wirusan city guards, large men who stood twelve-feet tall, even dwarfing Aum himself. Children no more than eight or nine years old stood as tall as Oadira, and pointed at the newcomers, giggling at how tiny they were.

As he walked, Aum stumbled to the ground, nearly passing out, but he was caught by his guards, who immediately helped him to his feet.

After a half hour of walking, looking up at buildings that made Oadira feel like an infant, they approached an oversized citadel made of marble stones so large no ten men could have ever hoped to lift them into place. A crowd of people had begun following them and swarmed around the steps of the impressive building.

Oadira and her entourage were greeted on the broad stairs by a gorgeous young woman who approached them smiling. Her chocolate-brown skin offset her royal, brownish-colored eyes. Her thick hair was pulled back into a tight ponytail adorned with golden hair accessories. On her slender arms, gold bracelets hugged tightly. She wore a flowing red dress that moved with the wind as she drew closer to the royal family.

"Welcome," the woman said. "The trees whispered of your coming several days ago. You are seeking Sahael. This is a blessing to us here in Wiruan. We have been at war with the Nazaummians for centuries; they are looking to eradicate the Wiru bloodline as they did Uzuri's Nadean bloodline. Your being here signifies the Signs of the Times are upon us." She paused and bowed to Oadira. "Excuse me, I'm the Educator to Ruler Aum who I'm sure failed to mention that the Narsans are trying to infiltrate the sanctuary with the help of the Nazaummian people."

"What is your name?" Oadira asked, as Lyshyla and the Educator made eye contact. She could only imagine the conversations these two would have, and how they would only ever share information with each other if the exact right question was asked at the exact right moment. It would likely be maddening to hear them speak to each other about something as pedestrian as the weather.

"My name is Lyla," the Educator replied. "It's an honor to meet both of you." Educator Lyla gave a soft curtsy, making eye contact with Lyshyla and hugging her for a brief moment.

Then a tall, elegant man seemingly glided close to the royal family and stood next to Educator Lyla. The sophisticated man introduced himself as Professor Adewara, a Lysinnian standing six-feet, nine-inches tall with ebony skin and pearl teeth.

"It's my pleasure to welcome you all to the great Wiruan city," Professor Adewara said. He bowed gently as Lyshyla quickly walked toward him and deeply embraced him, kissing him as they hugged and giggled.

"Thank you," Oadira said with a soft smile. In all their years as friends and allies, Oadira had never seen Lyshyla act that way before. Who was this man to her? They must know each other already. Did they have a romantic history? Questions churned as the professor pulled away slowly from Lyshyla's kiss.

"It's time for me to leave. I have to get to the Vannadale colony," Adewara said to Lyshyla. He quietly removed his arms from around her, hugged Lyla, and then turned away and disappeared into the crowd.

"Right now, we don't have the time to continue to speak openly," Lyla said, eyeing the crowd behind them. "The Ruler's life is nearly spent, and he needs a successor in place in order to pass on all of his knowledge to the next in the line."

Aum suddenly fell to his knees once again and was immediately taken inside of Wygir Palace to be attended to quickly.

The people from the crowd yelled, shouting to know what was wrong with their leader.

"The ruler has fallen ill," Educator Lyla cried to the people, "He will be taken care of as best we can. Now, disperse! Allow us to greet our guests properly and we will give you any updates on Ruler Aum's condition. Thank you all!"

The people grumbled and slowly moved away from the building, casting their massive shadows on Oadira and her family. Lyla motioned for them to follow her inside the palace.

"What's really going on?" Lyshyla asked as they entered the building. The ceilings rose at least four hundred feet overhead, with tapestries of gigantic size hanging against the walls. Giant animals and insects stood stuffed like statues among the pillars, each with detailed anatomical drawings and scientific descriptions beside them. Oya seemed particularly interested in the taxidermied wildlife.

"The ruler was poisoned by the Narsans," Educator Lyla said, voice echoing off the tall ceilings. "Your arrival was used as a distraction to poison the king somehow. Time is not on our side."

"How do you know it was our arrival that led to the king's poisoning?" Oadira asked. "We've only been with him for a little over a week, and we encountered no human enemies on our journey here."

"What's going on?" Lyshyla asked again, grabbing Lyla's

arm, forcing her to stop walking.

"The Line of Succession is to be upheld," Educator Lyla said while pulling away from Lyshyla's grasp. "Uzuri needs to be married. The Nairobi laws demand it!"

"What aren't you telling us?" Lyshyla asked.

"Uzuri needs to be married to a prince of royal lineage. All within your group possess royal blood," Lyla answered.

They followed the ruler to his personal chambers, where they placed him in his bed. Uzuri was at her father's side, holding his hands and looking at him as his body weakened.

Oadira watched the scene warily. How had an enemy poisoned Aum in the time since their arrival in this oversized land? It didn't make any sense. She remembered the king seeming very tired after they had spoken for the first time. None of this added up, and Oadira didn't like it. Plus, Lyla talking about Uzuri needing to marry someone of royal blood all seemed too convenient. These people wanted a savior and to return to Sahael. That was understandable. But was something more sinister afoot?

"Who would do such a thing, Father?" Uzuri asked as tears flowed down her eyes.

Aum breathed slowly; eyes closed.

"Someone who wanted your father dead, and the knowledge of the ancient Wiru people wiped out," Lyla replied, placing her hand on the princess' shoulder. "Something needs to be done about it as soon as possible."

The ruler's chambers filled with towering members of his council, worried about the Line of Succession and who the knowledge would be passed to next. They whispered about bloodlines and dying trees, acidic water, and their own place in Aarde. Some of the discussion made sense to Oadira, but some of it was completely foreign. She needed more information, and hopefully one of the large men and women standing over the king would let something slip.

"Can someone explain to me what's happening?" Oadira asked.

"The members of the council are here to see who Ruler Aum chooses," Lyla answered.

"Okay, so I'll take my family and leave you and his council," Oadira said.

"You can't!" Lyla said, practically jumping toward Oadira.

"And why is that?" Oadira asked.

"Because Ruler Aum has chosen your son Oxum, who is of the Orishan bloodline, a bloodline created by the Chosen and Ancient Blood," Lyla explained.

The Wiruan guards in Aum's personal chambers instantly marched over to Oxum and knelt in a show of respect. A confused look filled Oxum's face. He looked to Lyshyla and his parents for answers.

Oadira stepped in front of her son. "When did Aum make this supposed announcement?" she demanded. "We've been with him this entire time. Aum has never said a word to us about this, let alone had time to say it to you since we arrived."

"King Aum," Lyla said, eyes glancing from the floor to Oadira, "told me while…just before…"

"Stop," Lyshyla said. "You will tell my queen and empress the truth, now. Otherwise, we will find our way to Sahael on our own."

Nodding her head, Lyla motioned toward the door with her right arm. "Everyone, leave the ruler's chambers." She pointed to the council members and the gathered guard. "Leave us. The Orishan royal family can remain."

The gathered people nodded and made their way out the door. Only Oadira and her family remained with Lyla, Lyshyla, and Princess Uzuri.

"What I am about to tell you must not be mentioned outside these chambers. Is that understood?" Lyla said slowly. "A union between your son and Princess Uzuri would keep the Wirusan people united and the last Nadean half-blood as one. Without that, this people will splinter and fall apart."

"And why is that our concern?" Ozias asked, folding his arms.

"Because without the Wirusan," Lyshyla said, eyes closing slowly, "Entrance into Sahael is impossible."

"Why?" Oadira questioned, feeling suddenly hot and sweaty with anger. She stepped close to Lyla. "You knew about all of this before we arrived, didn't you? King Aum was already sick and dying. You're using us as an excuse."

Lyla seemed to shrink slightly. Her shoulders sagged and she looked at the floor. "Solomon told Aum that his time would be lengthened only until the return of the Orishan royal house to our lands. He's been sick for the past year, slowly growing weaker. We kept it a secret so the people would remain united. We planned to tell them he had been poisoned so they wouldn't give into despair and fear but be able to focus instead on a common enemy. Our people are hunted constantly by the Narsans and the Nazaummians. Death is our companion. We've held them together only through our king's will. If that will fails, the different families will break apart from each other and we will all lose everything."

"So, it's all propaganda," Ozias stated flatly.

"There's more to it," Lyshyla replied. "To enter Sahael, we need this people."

"Another prophecy," Oadira spat, stepping away from Lyla

and stomping her foot.

“The giants are a part of Sahael as much as anyone,” Lyshyla said. “They are the key to so much of the nation’s power and infrastructure. Without them, their strength and knowledge, we won’t even be able to get the gates open to let in the rest of our people.”

“Yes!” Lyla said, seemingly happy to have Lyshyla’s defense. “This people is key to the success of Sahael. If they are destroyed, any hope of victory against Natas and the Narsan disappears. That is why we need to unite the bloodlines here, as was promised, and pass Aum’s knowledge to the new sovereign. There would be the expectations of the new king and queen as they take on the Wirusan name forever.”

“Why is it you’ve chosen my son?” Oadira said.

“He’s of the Orishan bloodline and was chosen to help lead the people forbidden to leave Aarde to get to Sahael,” Lyshyla said. “As the selected leader, he won’t be able to leave this land.”

“What?” Oadira screamed. Aum jumped slightly in his stupor at the sound before returning to his delirium.

“That’s correct. Oxum has been chosen and is therefore forbidden to leave,” Lyshyla said.

“How is that fair to my family? This makes no sense at all,” Oadira said.

“It doesn’t, and it’s not fair,” Educator Lyla said. “But you have no choice in the matter. Your bloodline is bound per the Nairobi laws, created by the divines. And according to the Promise of Betrothal---”

“The promise can be bypassed,” Oadira shouted. “Oshún is proof of that. Educator Nortan gave him 80 days, of which we still have sixty-five left. You can give the same concession to Oxum.”

"But I won't," Lyla said with a nod.

"We'll see about that," Ozias seethed, neck muscles tightening.

"There's nothing you can do about it," Lyshyla said, putting her hand on Ozias' chest. "Your bloodline is bound. A vow of betrothal must be established so that a wedding in Sahael can take place."

"Another forced wedding, this time between Prince Oxum and Princess Uzuri?" Oadira asked as her voice elevated with each word.

"The vows of commitment need to be done so Ruler Aum's knowledge can pass to Oxum, binding Uzuri to him and the Wiru for time and eternity," Lyshyla said.

"My son didn't ask for any of this," Oadira said.

"How do you feel about this, Oxum?" Ozias asked.

Oxum looked at Uzuri. "I'm not…I mean…"

"Your bloodline is bound, or none of you will be able to leave," Educator Lyla explained. "You still must find a way to Sahael. It's what your bloodline has been cursed with, fixing the sins of those that came before you, prior to your bloodline being split four ways."

"You don't give orders to me and my family about where we can and cannot go," Oadira breathed, fists clenched. "You manipulated your people and brought us here only to take our choices from us."

"We all play a role in a bigger plan," Lyla said as a drop of sweat dripped down her temple. "Lyshyla knows this. Every Educator knows this."

Oadira's nose all but touched Lyla's. "And I'm tired of Educators playing god with my family. Perhaps we should find out what a king and queen of Sahael, along with their sons, can do against an army or Educators."

"I'll do it!" Oxum shouted, stepping forward. "I'll do it. I'll marry Uzuri and help others enter Sahael. I'll do it."

Oadira's mouth hung open for a second as she tried to speak, but no words formed. Ozias seemed stunned as well, though their sons smiled at their brother. Onika snapped his finger and pointed at his older sibling as if showing him respect.

"What do you mean, 'I'll do it?'" Oadira asked.

"You don't have to do anything you don't want to, Son," Ozias added.

Oxum glanced at Uzuri and smiled. "I want to." He stepped over to Oadira and took his mother's hands in his own. "Our whole lives we've watched you and Father sacrifice for our people. You've made choices that you didn't want to, so that one day no one will ever have to be enslaved or live in fear of tyrants. You taught us that we're part of something bigger than ourselves, and you can't tell me that if the situation was reversed, you wouldn't be willing to marry someone in order to avoid war and needless death. I know you would do the right thing, and now it's my turn to do so as well."

Oadira closed her eyes. Her sons had all grown into powerful and selfless men. She wasn't sure if she would make the same choice if she were in Oxum's place, but she knew she would have at least pondered the deal. A warm feeling emanated across the skin of her chest. She felt Okavango's Heart surge with power. The memory of her recent conversation with Ozias where she showed him the Heart came to her mind. Even if this was the only choice for her son, it was still his choice to make.

"It's different when it's your children," Oadira whispered, trying to keep tears from her eyes.

“I know,” Oxum replied. “But this is what we were all born to do. My brothers and I will serve, as you and our father have served.” He let go of Oadira’s hands and turned to Lyla. “I will marry Princess Uzuri and serve this people until they are able to return to the lands of their inheritance.

“Thank you for understanding, Prince Oxum.” Lyla said as she called for the counsel to reenter Aum’s personal chambers. “You are a credit to your family, and will be honored by this people, and the Educators of Aarde, long after your spirit has returned to the ancestors.”

The counsel returned and once again circled Aum’s bed. They all looked at Lyla with expectant glances.

“So, what’s happening now?” Ozias asked.

“The counsel needs to be present as the Oath of Promise is said by Prince Oxum” Educator Lyla informed. “They will escort Prince Oxum out of the room and speak to him individually, alerting him of the issues of the sanctuary, paving the way for Aum’s knowledge to fill in the gaps as his spiritual awareness enters your mind.”

“It’ll be alright,” Lyshyla said, ensuring Oadira that everything was going to be fine.

Aum’s condition continued to worsen as they stood there.

“He doesn’t have much time. If you’re going to do this, it needs to be done soon,” Lyshyla said.

“I’m not leaving my father’s side,” Uzuri said.

“Your father is going to be taken to the throne room so the ceremony can commence,” Lyla said. She looked at Oadira. “Such is our custom. If a king dies on his throne, he is given a special place in the Halls of Eternity. Aum deserves nothing less.”

The large Wiruan guards carried Ruler Aum to the throne

room and placed him on his dais. Aum slumped to the side against his armrest, coughing quietly. His skin had grown more and more pallid, as if he wasted away in front of them. Aum's council of rulers lined the hallways of the chamber. Prince Oxum followed closely behind with his brothers, mother, and father, being led by Lyshyla and Educator Lyla.

Everyone situated themselves inside of Wygir Palace in the Great Hall of Giants, a place where it was said the great giants were sent to Sahael to help defend the land to the death.

The royal family looked around the great halls of Wygir Palace as preparations were quickly made for the ceremony.

"The eyes of the Wiru statues look like ours," Oya said, bringing it to the attention of Lyshyla.

"That's correct," Lyshyla responded. "But the Nadean bloodline was one of the twelve tribes scattered during the fall of Sahael. They were eradicated. All that is left of their bloodline is Uzuri, and she shares the Wiru bloodline and is the last of the Nadean lineage. She is the reason the eyes of the giants are all sapphire. The people don't even realize it. They need to be brought back to Sahael. It's imperative that they are brought back to Sahael."

As the festivities started, food was placed on the table for the council, the royal family, and the most important people from the city, all in attendance. The council seemed eager to hurry and get the ceremony done as quickly as possible.

Lyla stood at the head of the table, eliciting a silence from the gathered mass. "It's time to begin. We're gathering here today for the sacred ceremony. We look to these two people to be betrothed and become one, uniting the Nadean bloodline with the Wiru lineage. This union will help complete the gathering in Sahael through marriage to solidify the ancient order that was established before the beginning of Aarde for time and all of eternity." Lyla motioned for Princess Uzuri and Prince Oxum to stand at the foot of the Ruler Aum's royal throne. "Both of you repeat after me: 'I take this oath with the goal of becoming the Ruler of Wiru's Sanctuary as I promise myself to the princess and the prince to me. I pledge to remain humble and open-minded and to honor the legacy of the Nadean bloodline who have come before me by paying it forward when we return to Sahael. I recognize my duty to adapt to the dynamic landscape of the sanctuary and to the tremendous growth with both palaces. I pledge to help each individual Wiru under my rule to the best of my ability, in line with the rules and the founding principles guided by the Nairobi laws.'"

Prince Oxum and Princess Uzuri repeated what Educator Lyla said, word for word.

Lyla held up a golden goblet full of wine. "To show your betrothal to each other, the last thing that needs to be done is for you both to jump over Nygir's broom and land on all four of your feet as one, being one in step with each in full equality as equals for time and eternity."

Everyone in the throne room rejoiced as the two royals leaped together over Nygir's broom and landed in unison.

"Let the prince and princess be married in Sahael for time and eternity, when that day arrives," Lyla shouted before drinking the wine. Another cheer filled the giant hall.

Oadira didn't know how to feel. She could see on her son's face that he was truly happy, especially when he looked at the lovely Uzuri. Still, so much of her life had been sacrificed, and she didn't want that burden placed on her sons.

"I know what you're thinking," Ozias whispered to her as the cheering continued.

"And what is that?" Oadira asked with a half-smile.

“You don’t want our sons to have to give up their choices like you and I did.”

“Maybe.”

Ozias put his arm around Oadira and held her close. “Oxum will be fine. Oshún will be fine. Both are now betrothed, and both made that choice themselves. Remember when we were told Oshún would need to marry Sy?”

“I do,” Oadira said, teeth grit.

“Do you remember what you said to me?”

“I remember you were angry.”

Ozias smiled. “I was. But you said you had chosen to marry me. You had chosen to sacrifice. You had chosen faith. What’s so different now?”

Oadira knew the answer, and didn’t even think before replying, “Because I don’t want my sons to be put in a position where they feel forced into anything. They’re my babies. I can’t let them go like that.”

“They aren’t going anywhere,” Ozias said, hugging Oadira even tighter. “They are being called as you and I were called. They are answering as we did. Their choices are theirs, and from the look on our son’s face, he’s pretty happy with his choice right now.”

Oxum grinned as he danced with Uzuri while people at the tables sang a song of celebration.

“He does look happy,” Oadira admitted. She looked at her husband. “I love you.”

“And I love you, my queen.” Ozias leaned forward and kissed his wife.

Immediately after the betrothal ceremony was completed, the sapphire eyes from the twelve giant stone statues lit up cerulean, spraying out Neelam mist that filled the throne room. Additional Neelam mist exited the ears of Aum as he gave up his spirit to be encompassed by the mist in the air as it mingled with the kings' mists of old. The mist entered back into the eyes of the Wiru kings, leaving a shared mist that entered Prince Oxum's cerulean eyes.

"Behold, great King Aum's spirit enters the undying realm!" Educator Lyla cried. "And his knowledge enters our new chosen ruler, King Oxum!"

As they feasted, Ruler Aum's body was burned before everyone, allowing his ashes to gather next to where the next statue would be built amongst the others that came before him. As the fire died down, Lyla informed the group they would retire to Aum's chamber for a discussion.

"I'll accompany you," Uzuri said as she finished placing the remainder of her father's ashes where his statue was to be built. She picked up the two Neelam stones from the center of the ash to be used as eyes for her father's statue.

Once everyone was settled in Ruler Aum's chambers, Lyshyla stood and spoke to everyone, looking Prince Oxum and Princess Uzuri in the eyes.

"The time has now come for both of you to lead these people to Sahael as Princess and Prince. Only when you return to Sahael to marry and consummate your marriage faithfully will Nile's flame infect every Wirusan, making them Orishan."

"I'd like an explanation as to why everything is happening at once," Princess Uzuri asked.

"The Signs of the Times are upon us," Lyshyla answered. "It was established from the beginning that the Ancient Order was responsible for the gathering of the ancient tribes that dwelled throughout all of Aarde and had the responsibilities of bringing them all back to Sahael. Before discussions of reaching out to find the lost tribes could take place, Lord Commander Natas and the Narsans infiltrated and destroyed Sahael."

Lyshyla paused and made eye contact with Prince Oxum and Princess Uzuri.

"The same is happening to this sanctuary. You are at war with the Nazaummians who have been trying to invade this place for centuries. The barriers are weakening and will crumble in time. You must hold on until it's safe to travel."

"We'll find a way," Educator Lyla said. "Uzuri and Oxum will help educate and prepare the people for the great migration across the Nazaummian lands."

"We would be putting the people in danger and in harm's way. It's why we must find a way to get our people to Sahael," Princess Uzuri said.

"I will do everything in my power to find a way," Educator Lyla said.

"We will stay in the sanctuary for now," Uzuri explained. "The barriers will hold as long as the power flowing through the Orishan bloodline remains strong. A migration of this size and magnitude will attract a lot of unwanted attention. We must travel through the Jilaum mountains; there is an inactive Nairohenge Gate that retracted back into the ground during the fall of Sahael. My father said that Nassir's three obelisks needed to be found and activated if the Nairostone Gates were to rise out of the ground once again. When active, the barrier protecting the sanctuary would no longer be needed, so long as the Ancient Bloodlines remain in Sahael."

Lyla nodded. "I will begin preparations at once and send the people to the Nairohenge Gates hidden in the Jilaum Mountains. The two of you will have to find a way to locate

Nassir's obelisks."

"My father told me of this often," Uzuri said as she took Oxum's hand. "This is a task that must be completed on our own. Once we have done what needs to be done, we'll find a way to Sahael."

"And what of us?" Onika asked. "Are we to do nothing while our brother searches?"

"You are free to find your way to the sacred lands," Lyla answered. Your family has its own path to follow now, and if you wish, you may draw attention from your brother's search at the same time."

"What's the best way out of the sanctuary?" Lyshyla asked.

"Salaum, one of our Wi scouts, will assist you," Princess Uzuri said.

"Thank you," Oadira said.

"We have a long trek ahead of us and must travel through hostile territory," Lyshyla said. "We will be pursued, and in so doing, it will take the pressure off of this place, allowing them all the time they need to prepare and travel west within the enclosed sanctuary."

Everyone gathered in the Great Hall before going their separate ways. Ozias and Oadira made eye contact with Oxum.

"My son," Ozias said. "I urge you to lead the people. There is much you will encounter before we meet again, but you must continue to find a way to get these people and your family to Sahael."

Lyshyla stepped forward and took Oxum's hands into her own. "Oxum, remember what I have taught you since you were a child. I have taught you all that is enclosed within the library of Timbuktu. As you come to realize the extent of the power that you have, that knowledge will be accessible whenever you require it. I have taught you everything about Aarde: its secrets and what it chooses to hide from all of its inhabitants. You and your brothers possess the Orishan gift of infinite knowledge. There will be times when you will not know what to do, but you will have to come up with a solution and you will know things that you previously did not. Thanks to your Ancient Bloodline and through the Dravidian Method of teaching, you will be able to recall all this knowledge when necessary. You will also be able to pass on this teaching method to your children, so that they can inherit all that knowledge as well from the library of Timbuktu."

"Once you have been taught something, you will always remember it. It is a gift and a curse handed down through the Orishan bloodline," Lyshyla explained.

"Why have you not mentioned this before?" Oxum asked.

"I have only mentioned it on three other occasions: when your mother and father were married, when Prince Oshún was betrothed, and now to you," Lyshyla replied.

"I understand," Prince Oxum nodded. "When the time is right, we will make our way toward the west. Before that, we need to prepare for all of this to take place, so we can devise a plan to avoid the violence the Nazaummians will bring into this city and upon the people they seek to destroy. I have heard in your teachings that if we were to circle their city seven times, we could make it fall upon our enemies. Is that correct?"

"Yes," Lyshyla answered. "But Oxum, such a feat would

be too great a risk to you and your people. That is something that you need to consider, and the importance of the role you will play in helping save your people and get them to Aarde.

"An untimely death by you would cause irreparable harm to Ishtar's plan. I do not think you could ever understand unless given time to have it manifested unto you like it has been to me. It is why you must find a way to get to Sahael as well."

Oadira stepped forward and hugged her son. "Good luck, Oxum. Always take care of your queen and treat her as the center of existence in your life. In doing so, she will make herself completely vulnerable to you and submit to you in ways you cannot even imagine."

Prince Oxum's eyes grew wet as he looked at his mother.

"*Tot ons weer ontmoet*, my child," Oadira told him. "That is the language of the Orishas, and you now possess the knowledge to speak it. We are the only ones who speak it when needed. It is your responsibility to educate your bloodline in our sacred language."

"I will, Mother," Oxum replied. "I do have one question for you that I wanted to ask. What is the language of Sahael?"

"Alkebulans," Lyshyla answered.

"I have heard that once all of the Ancient Bloodlines return to Sahael, the Sahaelian language will be shared among all of the Diaspora within Sahael," Oadira explained. "It will only be spoken by all the Alkebulans when they are in the presence of any royal bloodlines to ensure that their conversations cannot be heard or understood by outside influences. We must go, my son. *Tot ons weer ontmoet*," Oadira said as they embraced.

Oxum wiped his eyes and stood tall, like the king he now was.

CHAPTER IV

CARTHAGE ISLAND

Nazaum, Sanctuary, Carthage Island

"We have been traveling for three weeks," Salaum the guide said as he cut through a cluster of hanging vines with his machete. "I know you're all tired, but we're going to need to backtrack again."

Oadira groaned inwardly. They had been back-tracking, hiding for days on end, avoiding conflict, and trying not to engage those hunting them. Nazaummian trackers had found their trail after less than a week. Part of Oadira was glad because it meant these enemies would be less likely to stumble on Oxum and Uzuri's trail as they searched for the pylons to activate the gates, but it still made her family's journey that much more hazardous. Add to that the fact that her natural abilities were still hampered on this side of Aarde, and the mention of backtracking made her legs hurt even more.

"We're going to have to hide in the jungle and find a way down to the Maum," Salaum said as he wiped at his brow and readjusted the ponytail holding his braids in place. "From there we can travel alongside the river into the Expulsion."

"Can't we avoid the city of Maum if we continue across the dunes?" Lyshyla said. Her eyes were bloodshot. She seemed far more tired than the royal family. Still, she pushed on, never once complaining. "We know the Nazaummian are on our trail still," she continued. "We didn't lose them when we came out of the pass as we'd hoped. According to Lyla, the river is a straight path from here, and the fastest route."

"I had hoped for us to rest the night in Maum," Salaum replied. "We are all hardy individuals, but our bodies need rest. None of us have slept in three days."

Oshún came up beside Oadira and used his own machete to clear more of their bath. "And we won't be sleeping tonight either. I've been hearing animalistic yelping for the past hour in the distance behind us."

"I can hear hoarse barking sounds as well," Oya said, swiping at an insect in front of his face.

Oadira could now hear the barking too. She knew exactly what was making the sound.

"They're using Lope Mastiffs to track us," Salaum said.

"Lope Mastiffs are chasing after us?" Lyshyla asked. "I've never encountered one before."

"I have," Oadira said, feet crunching against fallen leaves on the jungle floor. "Imagine large, four-foot-tall dogs as big and as long as horses with the ability to smell from over two hundred miles away. They're fast, vicious, and your worst enemy. We can't rest because they can tell when we're awake and when we're sleeping, preventing us from keeping our distance between them. They don't sleep, rest, or need to eat for long periods of time to recover. They'll consistently gain ground on us. It's inevitable."

"Soon, they'll be mere miles away," Ozias agreed.

"Getting you all to the Expulsion is the only way to get them off of our trail to lose them permanently," Salaum said as he continued cutting a path in front of them. "We're in no condition to fight Lope Mastiffs, especially with your abilities affected. I'm a skilled fighter, but I wouldn't last two minutes."

"I can barely stand," Onika replied. "Even Oshún is stumbling along."

"Mind yourself, little brother," Oshún breathed.

"My legs are tired. Can we just rest for five minutes?" Oya asked.

"We have to keep pressing, and we're still hours away from the Expulsion. If we rest now, it'll all be for nothing," Salaum said,

"Salaum is correct," Oadira stated. She too felt deep fatigue due to the distance they had already traveled that day, coupled with the humidity and pestering insects. But she understood slowing down was not an option. "We can't stop boys. We're all suffering and needing sleep, food, and rest, but we must keep moving."

As evening approached, the group reached the end of the jungle. For the past hour, sand had started to encroach more and more frequently, covering the grass, and sucking the moisture from the air. Now they stood on the edge of a massive dune field with yellow waves of sand stretching to the horizon.

"The Lope Mastiffs are still a few miles behind us," Salaum informed as he knelt down and picked up a handful of sand. "We must enter the Expulsion to lose them and take our chances. Once we're in the river, we follow the flow of the current and get ready for a turbulent ride."

"I don't see any river," Oya said.

Ozias wiped sweat from his brow and nodded. "And once we enter the dunes, The Mastiffs will be on us in a matter of minutes. There is no cover out here, or any way to hide our tracks."

"It's now or never," Salaum said as he rubbed the back of his neck. "The river is over those dunes. It is still a ways ahead. We must run if we are to make it."

Lyshyla leaned over, hands on her knees. Oadira was afraid the woman might collapse.

"I can continue," Lyshyla said, holding her hand up toward Oadira as if to say she was fine. "Let's go."

Reluctantly, the royal family took off at a sprint. With each step Oadira's feet sank into the soft granules, forcing her to use more energy to pull out and continue running. Within minutes, every muscle in her legs burned. The group's pace slackened as they reached the first crest of a dune. In the distance she could hear water.

And the barking of Lope Mastiffs.

"They've found our tracks on the edge of the jungle!" Salaum shouted. He pointed behind them to a group of four Mastiffs less than a mile behind them. The large dogs took off in their direction at top speed.

"Run!" Ozias ordered.

It didn't matter how tired they were. Death approached, and any stumble or hesitation would allow it to catch up. They crested another dune, the sound of water growing louder and louder. The sun began to set, creating a beautiful sunset Oadira wished she had the time to sit and enjoy. She looked behind her but couldn't see the Mastiffs on the other side of the ridge. Still, she knew they were mere minutes from intercepting them.

"One more dune!" Salaum cried as he charged forward.

Barks could barely be heard over the rumbling of the river as they finally came to a rocky ledge that looked down on whitecaps and churning eddies. The Expulsion was a mass of twirling water smashing against jagged rocks. Under normal circumstances Oadira would try to find a safer place to enter the flow, but as she glanced over her shoulder and could see the saliva dripping from the Lope Mastiffs' mouths less than a hundred yards away, she knew there would be no safer entry.

"Jump, now!" Salaum shouted.

Everyone leaped into the Expulsion. Cool water hit their skin, but before anyone could get their bearings, the water twisted them away from each other. Oya was slammed into a rock and cried out painfully, but he remained conscious and tried to swim to Ozias.

"Use your gifts!" Oadira cried as she tried to keep herself afloat. "Our latent abilities still function well enough here! Swim and breathe!"

The royal family members blinked their eyes twice, activating their Orishan gifts and enabling their tattoo gills to appear under their ears so they could breathe underwater. Oadira dove beneath the surface, followed by Ozias and their three sons.

While under the churning water, Oya tried to help Salaum but was unable to grab hold of him as the current took the man in a different direction. Another current took Onika deeper underneath the water. He swam back to his family, pointing frantically downward. Oadira tried to swim to him, but a swirling eddy caught her and spit her upwards. Ozias grabbed her and before she could register which way was up, her head broke the surface and she breathed deeply. Ozias pulled her to a small gray sand beach beneath a cliff face. Oya, Onika, Oshún, and Lyshyla followed and were soon sitting beside Oadira catching their breath. The sky grew darker above them.

"I tried to save Salaum, but the current pulled him away," Oya coughed.

"He didn't have our gifts," Lyshyla confirmed. "I doubt he can survive this river. It is a sadness, but not one we can worry about now. Night is falling.

Onika stood and stepped back toward the river. He looked around frantically as if unsure what to do.

"Are you okay?" Prince Oya asked.

"Yeah," Onika nodded. "I was caught in the middle of several intersecting currents at the same time, but I saw a light glowing in the darkness deeper in the river where the currents slacked. I spotted several women trapped in obsidian chains at the bottom of the Expulsion sea floor. I thought they were dead, but then one of them opened her eyes, and suddenly I heard her voice in my head."

"What are you talking about?" Ozias asked.

"She spoke to me," Onika replied.

"We were only down there for moments," Oshún said. "What did she say?"

"It wasn't just words," Onika answered, eyes still on the rushing water. "It was like when Oxum was given the knowledge of King Aum. He suddenly knew things, right? That's what it was like. In a second, I knew things I shouldn't know. The seven women trapped down there were led by Mami Wata, the mermaid queen of the Black Mermaids. She needed help releasing herself so that she could release her six daughters. They're asking for our help."

Oadira looked at Lyshyla. "What do you make of this?"

Rubbing her wet chin, Lyshyla leaned forward and breathed deeply. "I know of the story, but the chances of us jumping into the river at the right place to discover them is almost impossible."

Ozias squeezed Oadira's hand tightly. "Nothing is impossible when you have faith," he smiled. "We know we needed to come this way to get to Sahael, but there were no other instructions beyond the truth that a path would be made beneath us even as we took our steps."

"Perhaps this is the path," Oadira agreed. "It's time for faith. We should release them and trust it is the right thing to do."

"They could be dangerous," Lyshyla warned. "According to the histories, Black Mermaids are not to be trifled with. They're dangerous."

Oadira looked at the water. "So are we."

Onika and Oya jumped back into the water and swam downward after a few minutes, they emerged. Appearing next to them was an unconscious young woman. Obsidian chains wrapped around both of her ankles that stretched back into the river. The woman was six-feet-five and had a chiseled physique and long, black, tiny-braided hair with long legs, and chestnut skin. She lifted herself up with both of her hands, coughing as she regained consciousness.

"What happened?" Ozias asked. "Did you free the Black Mermaids?"

"We did," Oya replied. "They spoke to us in our minds, just like Onika said they had. Mami Wata told me of the power of Onika's power of shout and to look for it at our greatest need. I'm having a hard time understanding what she meant. Other words and phrases were all mixed together. It was confusing, like a beehive of thought."

"But she told us to rescue this young woman," Onika said, helping the woman to sit up as she coughed and expelled water from her mouth. "She didn't tell us why or who she was, but we weren't going to leave her down there. Are you okay? Who are you?"

"I'll be fine. My name is Chimalsi," The woman replied.

"Why are you chained?" Oadira asked.

As Chimalsi opened her mouth to answer, a shout from above drew their attention. One hundred feet overhead on the rocky ridge, stood a dozen knights in the fading daylight, wearing exquisite armor. They sat on Percheron war horses in colorful harnesses and fine regalia. The men's shields and swords were drawn.

"This can't be good," Oya said.

"How many can you see?" Lyshyla asked.

Oya blinked his eyes, allowing them to glow and see better in the dark. "A dozen chevaliers on horseback and what looks like maybe a dozen soldiers standing between them on the ridgeline. They are all dark-skinned men with long, dreadlocked hair."

A knight in ebony armor dismounted his horse and began descending a steep path along the cliff that seemed invisible from where Oadira stood below. Another knight followed him close behind, sword at the ready. The Ebony Knight jumped the last ten feet onto the sand and stood tall before them as his companion followed.

"What brings you to the shores of Carthage?" the Ebony Knight asked.

"We washed up on the shores, emerging from the Expulsion from Nazaum," Ozias said. "We mean no harm. We were being pursued by Lope Mastiffs of the Nazaummians."

"They rescued me, Citewala, Sentinel Commander of Carthage," Chimalsi said, stepping forward.

A look of shock came to the Ebony Knight's face. He immediately dropped to one knee before Chimalsi. The Sentinel Knight did the same.

"Princess Chimalsi!" he cried. "You are alive!"

"Get us some horses, Citewala," Chimalsi ordered. "And cut these chains from my hands and feet. I will not be imprisoned again."

"Yes, my princess," Citewala nodded as he stood once again.

The knights led them up the path to the ridge. By the time they reached the gathered soldiers above, night had fallen. Oadira kept looking at Ozias, wondering what they were getting into. They had just rescued a princess by accident. Was that a good thing or a bad thing? She couldn't be sure, since this culture seemed entirely different from anything she had seen before.

Several of the Sentinel Knights quickly offered up their horses to Chimalsi and the group. Everyone seemed in awe of Chimalsi, as if she had just risen from the dead. They whispered and stole glances. Many of them seemed afraid.

"Please follow us back to the city," Citewala said as he climbed back on his large horse. "I am Sentinel Commander Citewala of Carthage. Duke and Duchess Chisulo are going to want to see you as soon as possible. I saw when we arrived that your eyes were glowing blue in the fading light. We've never had Orishans show up on our shores before; this is a rare occurrence. Most that travel through the Expulsion are caught below in the obsidian chains and are ripped apart by the intersecting currents. You've also returned with Chimalsi; I'd like to know how that's possible after so many years."

As the horses reared and turned toward the south, Oya pulled on his reins. "After entering the Expulsion and arriving on the Carthage shores," he began, "we found your princess trapped on the oceans floor in obsidian chains. My younger brother and I helped free her, Mami Wata, and Mami Wata's daughters."

Citewala stared at the princess as they continued riding. "We thought you had died at the hands of Natas."

"Natas?" Oadira asked. She pulled her horse closer to the leader. "Natas was here? When?"

"Twenty years ago," the knight replied.

"Twenty years!" Chimalsi shouted. Several of the horses jumped at her volume.

"What are you?" Prince Onika asked Chimalsi. "You were under the water for twenty years?"

"We will speak no more of this!" Sentinel Commander Citewala yelled at the top of his lungs. Again, the horses jumped. "We will make our way straight to the city. It is an hour ride. There your questions can be answered by those in authority who will not fall prey to superstitions and false prophets. The duke will explain everything when we arrive in Carthage. Silence for all, now!"

The order echoed through the rocky landscape and all chatter ceased. Again, Oadira wondered what they had gotten themselves into.

Stars blinked from above as they rode silently through this strange land dotted with lakes and rivers. Green Marula Trees sprouted everywhere. Firelight flickered in the distance and soon they approached a large city surrounded by stone walls as high as six men. Citewala gave an order as they approached, and the wooden gate opened for them.

Even in the dark it was obvious Carthage itself was exquisitely built from the finest stone, wood, and local materials. The city was vast, with shops, street venders, and nicely paved streets. Waterways crisscrossed the streets, passing under bridges and filled with boats and merchants. The canals seemed like busy thoroughfares and were decorated with murals and tile art. The people in the city started recognizing Princess Chimalsi and began to murmur among themselves, following the Knights to the Carth Palace.

Oadira rode close to Lyshyla. "What do you know about Carthage?"

"We are a people of water," Citewala said without looking at the two women. "If you want to know something, I will answer. You are our guests as far as I am concerned. Now that we are in the safety of Carthage, ask what you will of our province."

"Tell me about the city," Oadira smiled. "You seem to have skilled builders and an established trade foundation from all the shops. My studies have never focused on Carthage though, so I'd like to know more."

Citewala nodded. "Carthage is broken into four districts to help support the city, the people, and the local government. The Palace of Carth splits the city in half. It looks out over large bodies of water and our river systems. It has a great view. The royal family is able to see all types of fish, dolphins, harmless sharks, whales, and all types of sea creatures in the lake. We will be arriving shortly."

The Carthaginian people gathered around the Palace, eagerly wanting to get a glimpse of the lost princess. Gray stone, similar to the canyon where they jumped into the Expulsion, made up the walls of the citadel. Gold accents lined the windows with occasional murals and other works of art set into the stone made of what appeared to be shards of glass or gemstones. Lamps burned in the darkness, illuminating the entire area with expert precision. Canals led directly to the palace and disappeared into culverts for deliveries and transportation.

"This place is magnificent and inspiring, unlike anything

I've ever seen," Oadira said as she climbed off her horse along with the rest of their entourage.

"Wait here. I need to alert the duke and duchess," Sentinel Commander Citewala said. He ran up the steps past a pair of guards and disappeared into a hallway.

Oadira looked around, seeing how many more people were gathering around the palace. Many citizens started sitting in their boats as the streets and canals filled up with people trying to get a better view of what was happening. Even at this late hour it seemed the entire city remained alert and excited for whatever drama surrounded the castle.

"Everything is going to be alright," Princess Chimalsi said, waving to the bystanders as the light from the fires accented her dark skin.

The Sentinel Knights created a buffer between the people on the streets and the royal family and Lyshyla to ensure their safety. Chimalsi looked around at her citizens, glancing from the firelights in the surrounding buildings to the shadowed alleys. She seemed nervous.

"How are you doing?" Oadira asked.

"I'm not sure," Chimalsi answered quietly. "I was in a suspended state. I thought…I guess I don't know what I thought…or what I think."

Sentinel Commander Citewala returned with the duke, the duchess, and another woman dressed in royal robes. Another princess, perhaps? It had to be. She looked too similar to Chimalsi to be anything else.

"May I present Duke and Dutchess Chisulo and their daughter, Princess Chima!" One of the guards bellowed as the rulers ran down the steps.

Duke Chisulo was a large, old man with a white beard and

small, white afro. He stood nearly seven feet tall and looked magnificent, with his smooth chestnut, unblemished skin. Duchess Chisulo looked just as amazing despite her apparent age. She had a slender build with long white braided hair that went to the floor. Notwithstanding her white hair, she looked as young as Oadira. Princess Chima looked exactly like Chimalsi; they had to be identical twins. The only difference between them was that Chimalsi didn't wear earrings.

"Chimalsi! Chimalsi!" Duchess Chisulo said as she hugged her daughter as quickly as she could.

"Where have you been?" Duke Chisulo asked. "It's been twenty years!"

"It's a long story. I must have been trapped and suspended in time inside of the Expulsion," Princess Chimalsi answered. Tears came to her eyes as she hugged her father. "I have no other explanation."

"How were you able to stay alive?" Duke Chisulo asked, still embracing his daughter.

"I don't know. I was drowning. Natas and his men chained me and told me that because of our people's rebellion against him, I would suffer the agony of the water. They threw me in, but I found that suddenly I had glowing tattoos on my arms, and I could suddenly breathe. I panicked and tried to swim up, but I was chained. After a brief time, I felt suddenly at peace, and I closed my eyes. The next thing I remember was waking up on the sand bar with these Orishans."

"It's good to have you home after all of these years," Duchess Chisulo said.

The duke and duchess embraced Princess Chimalsi together. The princess turned and said 'thanks' to Oya who helped her to stand so she could hug her mother and father.

"You're so weak, my daughter," the duchess said, nodding to Oya in gratitude for his help.

"I see you've brought guests," Duke Chisulo said.

"Yes, they saved me," Princess Chimalsi said.

"We welcome you and your family to Carthage," Duke Chisulo said. "What can we do for you in repayment of this debt?"

"We are Ozias and Oadira, Rulers of Iceoth and Emperors of Neir's Realm," Ozias said with a bow. "These are three of our four sons, Oshún, Oya, and Onika. Our fourth son, Oxum, has recently been betrothed and is now King over the Wirusa of Nazaum. My wife and I seek your aid in our calling to enter Sahael and reunite the fallen bloodlines."

A gasp echoed through the gathering. The Duke and Dutchess glanced at their daughters and back at Oadira and Ozias.

"We've been waiting patiently for your arrival since Princess Chimalsi's disappearance," Duchess Chisulo said. "Part of the reason we fought so hard against Natas was because of our belief in the promised unification. Darkness cannot stand against light. We are descendants of the old bloodlines, promised to be brought back into the fold of one of the scattered Orishan bloodlines, after our only male heir left."

"Your lost heir?" Lyshyla asked.

"Yes, he will return soon, we know it." The Duke put his hand on Chimalsi's shoulder. "Our faith runs deep. We always knew Chimalsi was alive. We know her brother lives also. Even so, his birthright has been given to Princess Chimalsi. Her return is vital, allowing her to be next in line, and her sister Chima, third in line."

"Lord Commander Natas and the Narsans attacked you for reasons beyond your control," Lyshyla said. "There has to be another reason beyond simply your faith as to why they attacked

Carthage."

Duke Chisulo nodded his head. "Let us enter the palace and rest. It is late and the stars shine down. We will show you to guest quarters where a meal will be brought to you. Rest for the night and in the morning we can continue. You can ask whatever questions you have then."

Oadira could see in Lyshyla's bloodshot eyes that she deeply appreciated the Duke's offer. Once they had eaten, Oadira fell asleep immediately and dreamed of swirling rivers, giant dogs, and the shores of a country she hadn't seen since she was a child.

The following morning the group gathered in a sumptuous dining area with seven tables arrayed with golden candlesticks, cloths, and fine silverware. The Duke and Dutchess greeted them warmly and the meal commenced; all the while Sentinel Commander Citewala stood guard behind the royal couple. Chimalsi looked much healthier and in better spirits. She sat close to her sister as they whispered to each other and smiled. During Oadira's trials at Nereid's Monument she had lost several months of her life without realizing it. but to have twenty years taken away? That she could not fathom.

As the meal ended, Duke Chisulo began speaking with Lyshyla and announced to everyone they would respond to the Educator's every question so as to better help her and the royal family to enter Sahael.

"Many years ago," the Duke began after drinking the last of his fruit juice, "Lord Commander Natas and the Narsan fleet attacked Carthage, entering our great waters and bombarding us for months on end. They entered the four districts searching for members that shared ancient blood from Sahael, killing them one by one in each district. Many people had fled from the destruction of the continent 30 years before and had found refuge here. They had reestablished their lives and families. Natas wanted no survivors, and we were caught by surprise. My family was the only one left of the four districts that was able to avoid the Narsan soldiers and survive. Then Lord Commander Natas found my family after sending the full might of his naval troops to hunt us. We were safe until we lost Princess Chimalsi in all the confusion. Rumor spread she had been drowned to death, but we knew of our bloodline's rumored abilities to breathe underwater. Even so, when she didn't return, only our faith gave us strength in the hope she had survived. The Expulsion itself had only begun flowing ten years earlier, and we knew its power had carved the canyon and no one had survived swimming in its waters. Our fear was immense."

"Yes," Sentinel Commander Citewala explained. "I myself led our armies in search of the princess, but we found nothing after Natas left. Chimalsi is the last of the three bloodline heirs to the Carthinian throne thought to be killed or kidnapped at the hands of Lord Commander Natas and the Narsans. When they attacked Carthage, they went out of their way to kill all the heirs, knowing that the duke and duchess could no longer produce any more by Ibeji's blessings."

"Why is that?" Oadira asked.

"During the birth of our twins," Dutchess Chisulo began, "There were…complications that made our ability to sire children an impossibility. Chimalsi was our last hope." The Dutchess reached over and grabbed her daughter's hand. "We're so happy to see you," Duchess Chisulo said as she teared up, unable to speak.

Princess Chima's back stiffened in her chair, and she looked down at her empty plate. Oadira wondered why the rulers seemed to disregard their other daughter. The princesses were twins after all. If the Ancient Bloodlines ran in the veins of one, that same blood ran in the veins of the other.

Duke Chisulo wiped tears from his eyes. "We thought our daughter might never come back, no matter how strong our faith was. We started losing all hope, until we recognized the Signs of the Times as the currents reversed; we hoped they would bring our daughter Princess Chimalsi back to Carthage."

"We'd always hoped that we'd be able to return to Sahael one day," Dutchess Chisulo replied. "But those hopes were dashed when our son, Prince Abdul Chisulo, left using our most powerful ship to find his blood sister, and never returned. That has all changed now, with Princess Chimalsi's return restoring hope and a way back to Sahael."

Again, Princess Chima remained silent, eyes focused on her plate.

"I believe I understand the Expulsion was activated by Oadira after her eyes made contact with the waters in Iceoth," Lyshyla said. "You mentioned it has only flowed for what, thirty years at this point? That lines up with everything else from the prophecies. It's why the Expulsion enabled all of us to get to Carthage's coasts safely. It's the only reason why Princess Chimalsi is here now on your shores once again."

"It's been decades since an heir was in Carthage. Because of that we've had to keep Chima, our adopted daughter, under constant guard every day," Duchess Chisulo said.

"Wait, she's not your blood daughter?" Ozias asked.

"She and Chimalsi look exactly the same," Oadira replied. "I assumed they were twins."

"I am not of the bloodline," Chima said quietly, never looking up."

"That's a secret we've had to keep within our family circle for decades," Duke Chisulo said. "As kings and queens, you understand the politics involved in ruling. We needed to make certain arrangements to guarantee the survival of our bloodline. You understand."

Oadira understood but didn't like it. The Duke and Dutchess may not have wanted to say it out loud, but Chima was a decoy, pure and simple, meant to die in place of Chimalsi should the need ever arrive. Natas would not have been fooled by such a stratagem though. Chima must have lived the last twenty years knowing her adopted mother and father wished every day it had been her to disappear instead of Chimalsi.

They were interrupted by a large man standing six-feet-eight, with a smooth bald head and no facial hair.

"Ah, Educator Cantor," Duke Chisulo said "There is much more to discuss. Come follow me, and we'll converse inside the council chambers. We can discuss much more there."

After settling into the council room with its circular table and windows that looked out on the city below, Educator Cantor brought up Nephrophida's interactive map, which shifted and moved as he touched it.

"As you can see here," Educator Cantor said, "the map now shows possible locations of scattered and dispersed tribes throughout Aarde. We have kept track as well as possible through our trade routes in hopes of finding all of them."

Looking closely at the map, Oadira noticed the scattered Orishan tribes were in the exact locations that she and her family had all visited over the past 30 years.

"After the fall of Sahael," Educator Cantor continued, altering the map to show the continent of Alkebulan, "the bloodlines were scattered by Lord Commander Natas and the

Narsans. They were dispersed all over eastern and western Aarde. Many of them were able to escape and thrive, hence the creation of Carthage, created by those that share the Chosen and Ancient Blood. The Orishan bloodline was scattered that terrible day along with the other three bloodlines.

"Nephrophida's map shows Carthage's influence on this side of Aarde. We possess all the naval supremacy and power of the open seas. But since Nata's attack 20 years ago, we've been relegated to just this island and the waters within it. Carthage is a nation built on clean waters that sustain the population. We are a strong and up-and-coming nation, but we have been prevented from ruling the open oceans once more because we can no longer leave our own waters."

Nephrophida's map shifted once again, showing Carthage, Nazaum, and the surrounding waters.

"There is dark water and ash that surrounds all the lands on this side of Aarde," Cantor informed, pointing at the oceans surrounding the land. "They prevent us from traveling because of the obsidian ash that has caused destruction to our rebuilt fleet. Dark water is slowly eating away the lands it touches. We're looking for ways to see how it can be corrected."

Duchess Chisulo stood and pointed at the landmass and an inscription showing the city of Carthage. "After establishing our presence, we found symbols depicting the existence of a people that dwelt here long ago."

"Yes," Lyshyla agreed. "This I have knowledge of from the records of Timbuktu. Many years ago, a fraction of the Orishans dwelled in Carthage, and an agreement was established with Ishtar and Obatala, who sent their firstborn children to Sahael to learn the Kemettian artes of the ancients. As part of that agreement, those royal families were ordered to destroy all remnants of that history nearly four hundred years ago and to not leave any trace for Lord

Commander Natas and the Narsans to find."

"Now that I've caught you up on our history, there is an urgent matter that needs to be discussed with the royal family," Educator Cantor said.

"Prince Oya," Duke Chisulo said as everyone stood. "Would you mind escorting Princess Chimalsi to her quarters? She is still weak from her ordeal."

"Of course, Duke Chisulo," Oya nodded.

Everyone left the counsel room except for Oadira, Ozias, Onika, and Lyshyla. Duke and Duchess Chisulo and Chima stayed seated as the guards and servants left.

"What do you want to discuss with us that's so urgent?" Lyshyla asked.

"A way to clean and remove the dark waters forever from this side of Aarde," Educator Cantor said. "We are a people of water, as you have seen. We know it is a Sign of the Times and that somehow Queen Oadira is responsible, as you said earlier. We need these waters healed if we are to survive."

"How is that possible?" Lyshyla asked.

"There is a way," Dutchess Chisulo assured.

"Many years ago, at the time the currents started reversing on this side of Aarde, the waters of Carthage City began to brighten and regain life," Educator Cantor said. "This caused the ash to dissipate entirely and creating a protective layer around the island. Many years ago, I swam down to the bottom of Carthage City's seafloor and noticed Nephrophile's kyanite stone emanating with small waves, restoring life to the island.

"Nephrophile's kyanite stone had within it his trapped memories and histories about our ancestors. Nephrophile's knowledge in the form of mist after Chima and I cracked the kyanite stone entered Nephrophida's interactive map. Nephrophile's mist revealed a way we could regain control of our seas and remove the liquid obsidian water that surrounds Carthage and all of the other side of Aarde."

Chima nodded, standing tall for the first time that morning. "From the center of Carthage Lake, we were able to retrieve treasures that would be able to play a part in cleansing these waters permanently."

"Please follow me to Carthage Hall. Everything discovered from Carthage Lake is there," Duke Chisulo said.

"How were you able to retrieve these items?" Lyshyla asked.

"Chima was able to swim down to the bottom and retrieve them individually," Educator Cantor said. "She was invaluable."

Chima smiled.

"Chima and Educator Cantor retrieved most of what was thrown in the open water area and placed them in their great hall," Duke Chisulo said. "Please, follow me."

They made their way to the great Carthage Hall across the city square and the primary bridge. The hall was vast, made of white, chalky, pure stone that absorbed sunlight rather than reflecting it. The inside was adorned similar to the palace, though instead of colorful murals of stone and glass, threaded tapestries hung, covered in historical drawings that included Nata's attack. Oadira looked up at the dark-skinned man with his red eyes and glowing crimson tattoos. She wanted to spit on the tapestry and burn it. The interior walls were made of transparent glass as were the floors, which were filled below with water that had fish swimming through them like a massive aquarium. Water flowed throughout the great hall.

After entering a side chamber, Educator Cantor walked

them to a central table covered in artifacts large and small. Sapphire anchors, plugs, and gold bars sat among other treasures of curious design.

“We need your assistance to help restore trade and commerce in the back parts of Aarde,” Educator Cantor said. “When we were in the council room looking at Nephrophida’s interactive map, you saw how commerce affected the surrounding continents. We need to ensure Carthage can reestablish trade with these struggling nations.”

“Why is this so important?” Oadira asked.

“Without our ships, the back half of Aarde will die, along with the other continents that are depending on us to bring food, medicine, and supplies. Plus, it helps offset the power of the witans and Nata’s armies. Carthage is responsible for all the life that dwells in these seas: the fish, whales, turtles and all other creatures that keep Aarde’s waters clean. The dark waters are moving closer to Carthage, and the barrier is weakening as the seafloor pushes sea life to the bottom, threatening all life on this side of Aarde. It’s imperative that one member of your bloodline stays to see this side of Aarde cleansed and liberated against the threats that seek to destroy it.”

“I understand the problems that you all are facing, but at this moment we cannot help you,” Oadira said, looking at Ozias, who gave his approval. “We’re doing all that we can to get to Sahael. The black waters surrounding this island will be kept at bay.”

“We know of your royalty,” the Duke said. “We know of our faith. We know the prophecies. Our bloodlines are to reunite. You cannot tell me that your coming here and finding my daughter was a coincidence. It was the will of Ishtar himself. Am I wrong, Educator Lyshyla?”

Lyshyla looked at Oadira and swallowed. “You are not,

Duke Chisulo. We knew our path ran west and that we would be led to the lost Nairohenge Gates on this continent. As we've traveled, we've encountered remnants of the people of Sahael and reunited with them. Two of the royal sons have been drawn to princesses and been betrothed. I'm assuming that's what you are implying here as well."

Dutchess Chisulo looked at Oadira, eyes pleading.

Oadira took a deep breath. Since leaving Neir's Realm, her family had been on a path of slowly splitting apart. They had already left Oxum behind, and Oshún would return to Sanctuary to be with Sy in less than forty days. Onika was still shy of 17 years old, so Oya would be the sacrifice in this case.

As if reading her thoughts, the Dutchess began speaking. "Your son, Oya, seemed quite taken with our daughter. Would he be willing to join our house and reunite the bloodlines for the good of Sahael? We know this is fast, being as how you only arrived last night, but such arranged marriages have always been common."

"And no faster than our other two sons' betrothals," Ozias murmured.

"It is a great thing you ask of my family and my son," Oadira stated, back straight. "But, as long as my son, Prince Oya, is willing, he can remain here, betrothed to your daughter. The power stored within this island will grow until you have found a way to restore the waters on this side of Aarde."

As Oadira spoke, Prince Oya and Princess Chimalsi walked into Carthage Hall holding hands. They were escorted to meet up with everyone else.

Oadira approached Prince Oya. "My son, I have seen the way she looks at you and the way you look at her. It's only a matter of time. We've been traveling for nine months, and I've learned letting you all go is the only way you'll grow up to see the realities of Aarde. You and your brothers come from a godly bloodline with elite talents, gifts, and supreme intelligence. When the two of you are married in Sahael, during your consummation Nile's flame will infect the Carthaginians bloodline, giving you, Prince Oya, full and complete control through the Chosen Right of Election; allowing the king to take over the Carthaginians bloodline. Is this something you would choose."

Oya smiled at Princess Chimalsi. "The two of us have been discussing this very thing. We know it was the will of the gods that we found her yesterday, and both of us are aware of the unifying of the bloodlines. Obatala and Ishtar are in all our movements, Mother. Ever since you were born, the heavens have swirled with anticipation. I will stay here and be betrothed to the princess, and she to me. Such is our part in all of this, and it's a part I choose gladly."

After speaking with Prince Oya and Princess Chimalsi, Oadira addressed everyone in Carthage Hall.

"It's inherently in the blood of all the Orishan people within the Chosen Bloodline to rule and give grace to the people of all Aarde. It's your people who were enslaved to keep the ancient knowledge within our lineage suppressed. Lord Commander Natas and the Narsans have empowered enslavers to be more powerful by using the strength of your bloodline as a means to build their countries and profit at your expense."

"It's imperative our family gets to Sahael as quickly as possible, but I ask you to make me one promise," Ozias said.

"Yes, Father, what is it?" Oya asked.

"Once your seas are cleared, you're going to want to begin trading and helping the others that need food and goods to help sustain themselves. I urge you to plead with those who would want this side of Aarde for themselves, even if it means going to war with them and bringing them to heel. They're being controlled by the Narsans," Ozias said.

"How do we break that control?" Oya asked.

"To ensure their control was everlasting, they used Nassir's three obsidian obelisks to regain that control after taking them from Carthage," Lyshyla added. "The same obelisks your brother Oxum is searching for with his future bride. You must search as well."

"I accept this mission," Oya stated. "And we will all be united in Sahael."

Oadira walked over to the table and picked up one of the artifacts that had been pulled from the ocean floor. "There is only one major problem though," she said. "As Educator Cantor told us, to the west, toward Sahael, the water has become impassable due to the obsidian ash. Without the Nairohenge Gates, there is no way to cross the ocean without our ships being torn to shreds."

"Yes," Chisulo nodded. "And the only place to find refuge in that area is Nartica Island, which was ravaged by Natas when he attacked Carthage 20 years ago. Nartica was always the last stop for sailors coming to Sahael from the east. Sailing the currents is almost impossible unless you already know the way to the holy continent. You will need to enter the center of Nartica through the gates and find whatever maps you can find, otherwise you'll never make it to Sahael."

"Maps won't help us if we can't even sail to the island because of the corrosive ocean," Oadira replied.

"The queen is right," Lyshyla said. "We have to find a way to cross the obsidian, ash-infested black waters that cover the back half of Aarde."

"I know how to get across the dark waters. My Sec-birds could assist you," Chima said as she grinned from ear to ear. "I've been thinking about it as a way for merchants to explore the waters, but it could work for this as well."

"How?" Oadira asked.

"What is a Sec-bird?" Ozias questioned.

"Large birds that have the ability to walk across or glide across obsidian, ash, and dark water," Chima continued. "Many years ago, when they were little birds, they got out of their cages and made their way onto water. I thought they'd die instantly from the ash, but that didn't happen. That's when I knew they could be of use one day. I'll take you to where they live. Follow me."

They all followed Chima to the small area in Carthage Palace where she kept a pool of dark ash water. The liquid was black, with what appeared to be sharp slivers of obsidian throughout. Chima's Sec-birds had their nests built on top of the black water combined with liquid obsidian and ash. Chima placed one of her Sec-birds in the black water, and just as she said, nothing happened to the small fluffy chick. They were able to resist the effects of the blackwater, providing the royal family with an option if traveling across the dead sea.

Everyone gasped in amazement.

"Chima, this is wonderful," Duke Chisulo grinned.

"I've been coming up with ideas on how to use them, but I wasn't sure it would be a good idea," the princess said. "Fully grown Sec-birds can carry a rider. Normally they are too wild to carry a passenger, but the Sec-birds in our menagerie are trained. They can fly for some distance before landing in the water unharmed by the particles. They can take the royal family on the air currents until they've crossed the sea."

Dutchess Chisulo hugged her adopted daughter. "You are full of ideas. Never forget that."

"We can continue traveling to Sahael," Oadira smiled. "We haven't been here long, but it's imperative we leave as soon as possible. We're so close, and I won't waste another day."

"Before we depart, there is something you must do for us," Lyshyla said. "Once these waters are cleared, do all you can to create trade with the Triennium. Mask your ships to travel among them and learn of their shipping routes."

"And continue to develop your Orishan abilities, especially your shape-shifting abilities, to mimic the people that you will be among," Oadira said to Oya. "It's not something you've needed to use up until now, but it will be a help to you as you search for the obelisks."

Prince Oya nodded confidently, agreeing to his mother's counsel.

"Do Carthaginians have marriage ceremonies?" Ozias asked.

"No," replied Educator Cantor. "They are betrothed and then married by both the Duke and the Dutchess in Sahael according to the Nairobi laws. The betrothal process is fast. Would the both of you like to complete it now? Then, when we get to Sahael, you both can be properly married."

"Are you two certain you want to promise yourselves to each for time and eternity?" Oadira asked.

Oya looked at Chimalsi.

They both nodded their heads in agreement.

"Very well," Educator Cantor smiled. "Allow me to recite the Oath of Engagement; afterwards, repeat the same phrases word for word. 'I take this oath with the goal of becoming the best spouse I can be for my mate. I pledge to remain humble and open-minded and to honor the legacy of leaders past who have come before me by paying it forward in the same Carthaginians tradition. I recognize my duty to adapt to the Signs of the Times to help increase growth in the people. I pledge to help each individual

Carthaginians entrusted to my care to the best of my ability, in line with the founding principles centered around the Nairobi laws.'"

Prince Oya and Princess Chimalsi recited the vows to each other, betrothing themselves and agreeing to consummate their marriage when they returned to Sahael.

The royal family left after less than a week without a royal send off. Their farewell with Oya had taken place the night before. It was then that Oshún told them he would be leaving as well. Forty-three days had passed since they left Sanctuary, and he knew it would take him that long to return. An emissary from Carthage was leaving the next day by ship to visit Sanctuary, and Oshún would be going with them. Tears were shed, particularly on the part of Onika, who now would be the only prince remaining with his parents.

"Have faith, little brother," Oshún had said as he and Oya stepped back toward the palace. Oadira wiped at her tears, praying she would see her sons again in the restored lands of Sahael.

As Ozias and the boys went to gather the Sec-birds for their flight, Oadira sat in the courtyard as the sky slowly brightened in the east. The pack on her back was heavy with supplies for the journey, but the weight over her heart seemed greater. She pulled Okavango's Heart from beneath her traveling robes and held the large blue jewel in her palm. The gold chain tugged at her neck. Here was the power of life itself, a power that would help them enter Sahael in some unknown way. Such a small thing with such a big job.

It reminded Oadira of herself.

And her sons.

Small things being called upon to perform miracles for millions of people. Was she up to the task? Were her boys? It was too late to ask such questions. They were in the middle of their journey and couldn't back out now. She put the Heart back against her chest and felt the weight of the chain again.

It was a weight that would only grow heavier in her mind as they traveled over the next few weeks.

She, Ozias, Onika, and Lyshyla departed quietly from the center of Carthage before the sun had risen. They were rested and restored, with provisions provided by the Duke and Dutchess in leather packs on their backs. They climbed on the backs of their Sec-birds as the large creatures flapped their massive white wings and took off into the air. The Sec-birds reminded Oadira of oversized herons, or pelicans she had seen flying next to the ships the LaLaurie sisters would take to the Royal Rumble each year. The massive birds flew low over the dark water, following the flow of the current. Every half hour or so they would land on the sea and rest, naturally repelling the damaging properties of the dark water.

"Chima cautioned that we're not to deviate from the current or risk being caught by the lighthouse that is positioned to catch all things within it," Lyshyla said to everyone as the birds caught their breath. "She said her Sec-birds will follow the flow of the current, no matter the circumstances. This will be a long trip, so be alert and stay focused at all times and hold close to your Sec-bird. This is the open sea."

While traveling, they saw death everywhere below them. carcasses of killer whales, blue whales, and large alligators floated in the water. The smell made them all dizzy as they observed flying crickets eating the dead flesh and then laying eggs inside the rotting sea creatures to multiply since they had a food source.

Large water snakes traveled through the dead whales as they burrowed holes in the underbelly of the decaying creatures.

They could all see floating dead fish around the carcasses, permeating the air. The Dead Sea had truly earned its name.

After traveling several hours, they became lost in a rising mist. The air current seemed to stall, and the birds landed, squeaking as if confused.

"Where are we?" Oadira asked.

"In the middle of nowhere," Lyshyla said.

"So, we're lost?" Onika said.

"It's this mist," Ozias shouted. "I can't see anything. It's like the winds and currents simply stopped. Should we swim under and see what we can see?"

"The sec-birds can't breathe underwater," Lyshyla informed. "If we are out of reach of them, the tiny shards of obsidian will cut us to shreds as easily as they do the ships that flounder in this water. We need patience."

Suddenly, a figure appeared in the distance through the mist.

"I see something approaching from the sky. It's Chima," Onika said to everyone.

A bird landed in front of them, and sure enough, just as Onika had said, Chime rode on the fowl's back.

"Why are you here?" Lyshyla asked.

"I snuck out of the palace," Chima said.

"The Duke and Dutchess will be worried sick," Oadira said.

"I'll be fine, not to worry, I'll be home before they wake," Chima said.

"So, where do we go?" Onika asked.

"Just follow me. I'll help get you all across the dead sea," Chima said.

"Are you sure?" Oadira asked. "Do you know where to go? Have you ever made this journey before?"

"It's my destiny to accompany you all through the dead sea. I have to save my family at all costs," Chima said.

"I understand," Oadira replied. She understood the woman's drive. After coming in second her entire life, even when her 'twin sister' was presumed dead, Chima wanted to prove her worth. This was her way of doing it.

Chima patted her Sec-bird's feathers. "We have to be careful at the top of the four lighthouses. There are windlances laced with large, white arrows with gold tips that are fired through the gray clouds. They're undetectable, so caution is needed. Many of our sailors have seen bird-riders taken down by these means. We must keep our heads on a swivel in case one of them is shot in our direction."

The group took to the skies once more. After flying smoothly for some time, Chima informed the group, "We're halfway there."

"How can you tell through the mists?" Onika shouted.

"Keep following me," Chima yelled. "Don't deviate to the right or the left out of formation."

With the wind pressed up against her face, Oadira did as instructed. Her family followed her lead.

After another hour they passed through the mists into the shining sun. in the distance Oadira could see a large landmass made of pure ice with permanent snow fall throughout the whole area. Towering cliffs of glacial snow rose over the dark ocean.

“We’re close,” Chima called to the group. “This is Nartica Island. We still must travel inland though. I checked the maps, and we should continue to head west.”

As they moved further into the continent, the surface below changed from snow to black charcoal and ash. The air currents grew stronger, pushing the birds along. Their wings flapped frantically and Oadira could tell her mount grew increasingly weary. Then, as the sun drew high in the sky, Lyshyla shouted.

“Look below!”

The current had led them to a series of black stone cliffs two hundred feet tall. Reflecting the sunlight were two double doors that were easily each thirty-feet wide and at least that tall. The birds descended swiftly, clawed toes scraping against the pebbled ground. Dismounting, Oadira and Ozias approached the doors, which appeared to be made of charcoal. Strange silver writing and carvings adorned the dark surface. Wind blew hard across the barren land. No trees or plants of any kind could be seen all the way to the horizon.

“There is writing on the charcoal doors,” Lyshyla said.

“What does it say?” Oadira asked.

“I can’t make out what it says,” Lyshyla said. “I’m unfamiliar with the symbols, but they appear similar to the ancient texts of the Kemites, though bastardized and altered.”

“It reads ‘The Neutral Zone: Those who enter must give life to preserve neutrality,’” Chima said as she translated the silver text. “This is the old script of my people. Few can read it today, but those of the royal house still study it.”

“How do we get the large doors to open?” Lyshyla asked,

“Are we sure we want to open these doors?” Onika asked. “I’ve never known us to have a good experience by walking through a strange door. Oya loves to tell me about the Treep

Spiders."

"Blood will be required to leave this place," Chima said under her breath. "The blood of royalty must be shed to turn the locks and enter the Neutral Zone. Please hand me a dagger."

"I have one," Ozias said. He pulled a dagger from his belt and handed it to Chima. "You said it needs royal blood. I can do it."

"No," Chima said. "It will be me."

"You are not of royal blood," Lyshyla said, shaking her head. "You were adopted into the Duke's house."

Chima turned to Lyshyla, face stoic. "There is more to royalty than bloodline. Royalty means sacrifice and honor. I do not believe you are born into either of those things. I am royal because I make the choices a royal should make. Now stand back."

With the dagger, Chima cut her right and left palms. She squeezed her fists closed to promote blood flow and walked over to the dirty, charcoal gates. She closed her eyes for a brief moment, said a prayer, and placed her bloodied hands on the cold, black stone, rubbing downward. She stepped back and stood next to the family as everyone watched the dark-red handprints stand out in juxtaposition to the stark-black gates.

Oadira held her breath, waiting for an unknown sign. After a few seconds, the bloody prints started to shrink, as if absorbed into the rock. Once completely immersed, a small aquamarine Paraiba Tourmaline light appeared at the top of the left door. Slowly, the light elongated and continued to grow as it traced the perimeter of the barrier, leaping to the second door. In a matter of seconds, the entire gate was outlined in a powerful blue light. The ground shook and rumbled as the gates parted. Rocks tumbled from the cliff and shattered mere feet from Oadira's family.

"Hurry and enter as the doors are opening!" Chima

ordered. "Once they're fully opened, they will swing completely shut quite instantly. Leave the birds."

"No, they'll come with us. They can rest as we travel through this place," Oadira ordered.

"Understood," Chima replied. "Get ready!"

CHAPTER V

NARTICA ISLAND

The other side of Aarde, Nartica

They entered through the large charcoal doors. Just as Chima had warned, they swung shut from behind them with a deafening boom that echoed through the cavern now before them. It was so dark, even Oadira's power of dark vision did nothing against the pitch.

"I can't see anything!" Onika shouted. His voice bounced around, evidence of the space's size, but giving no other details.

"I have something," Chima said. The sound of her rustling in her bag seemed far louder than it should have been. Then, a pale light appeared in her hand and grew brighter until the walls of the cavern became visible all around them. Black stone and ice were everywhere, a solid wall of it on both sides of them. The ground below led down a narrow path, where the air was cold with no taste at all.

"You have an Illumination Orb," Lyshyla grinned. "They are quite rare."

"It was given to me years ago by Educator Cantor," Chima informed. "It charges in daylight and can glow for several hours. It will weaken though, so we should move quickly."

Onika looked around them and breathed deeply. "So much for you making it back before your parents wake up."

Chioma smiled. "I knew that would never happen, but if you had known, I feared you wouldn't have let me lead you."

"We are glad you are with us, Chima," Oadira said, touching the woman's arm.

"You truly are of royal blood, no matter what anyone else ever says," Ozias smiled.

"I never knew a place like this could ever exist," Lyshyla said as she walked up to the walls and placed her hand on a large icicle. "In the future, we'll have to find a way to get our Educators inside of this place."

Chima nodded. "We're in Nartica. Everything is made of pure Narthax ice, an indestructible substance that never melts no matter how hot it gets. Narthax never goes away."

"How did this place get here? I've never seen it on any of the maps nor in Timbuktu," Oadira asked.

"I know why," Lyshyla answered. "It wasn't verified in Timbuktu. This island was created when parts of the asteroid that entered Aarde's atmosphere broke off into many pieces. This place used to be just a small land mass of ice. After the asteroid made contact with it, this place expanded into what it is now."

"Where are we?" Ozias asked.

"We're in the center underground in an icy tunnel created over five hundred years ago, after the ancients descended upon Aarde making it their home," Chima replied.

"What more can you tell me about this place?" Lyshyla asked Chima.

"Much like you said, after the Kemites arrived in Aarde, many of them left Alkebulan to make a life for themselves. They traveled in every direction to make and create their own settlements all over Aarde, until they were hunted down and destroyed by the Narsans. The Narsans found those places and killed as many Kemites as they could. The Neutral Zone is what separates upper and lower Nartica to keep the peace between the nations."

"I would've never thought that a neutral location was needed to prevent war between two nations and to keep the peace," Ozias said.

"The Neutral Zone was also created by the Kemites when Natas was cast out of the presence of Ishtar and Obatala," Chima continued. "My father the Duke made me study so no one would ever doubt my parentage. I know much about these lands. It was initially created for their Black children as a place of refuge to escape witan terror and persecution for enslaved runaways. There were other Kemites sent down to Aarde to dwell in upper and lower Nartica. They intentionally descended to keep a watchful eye on Lord Commander Natas at all times, before they were destroyed by the Narsans. That wicked army now uses it for their own means. Under Ishtar and Obatala's orders, this remnant of that people, the few who survived, were commanded to leave the Neutral Zone and make a home in the Holy Land of Alkebulan secretly, to preserve their lineage."

"I understand," Lyshyla said. "But allow me to fill in the remaining details. You did not mention that they left this place and made their way to Sahael also."

"No!" Chima protested. "That's wrong according to some of those that still live in upper and lower Nartica. The Kemites who lived here are the ones who kicked the Narsans out of Nartica, surgically preventing them from ever having a foothold on this other side of Aarde."

Oadira looked from one woman to the other. It felt good to

see someone challenging Lyshyla's knowledge.

"I had no idea that these Narsans tried fighting the Kemites to control the other side of Aarde," Lyshyla said, rubbing her chin. "The Narsans wanted the strength to invade all of eastern Aarde and eventually Sahael. There was always a group that worked in the shadows on behalf of the divines, preventing Aarde from being whitewashed as it was a gift to the Black inhabitants."

"That is correct," Chima said, nodding her head in agreement.

"Aarde was a refuge for Black people? What about the witans? Why are they here in the first place?" Onika asked.

"To ensure the safety of all Blacks, Ishtar and Obatala had to send witans, to determine where the threats facing their children would be coming from," Chima answered. "After fifty years of war, the divine Kemettian population was decimated and reduced by fifty percent. They were barely able to maintain control of Nartica after twenty-five more years of Narsan attempts to reclaim Nartica. The Narsans finally stopped vying for control of Nartica. If they had gained control here, a war for Alkebulan and Sahael would've taken place."

"So, they just continued to fight?" Lyshyla asked.

Chima nodded her head. "After their final skirmish, the Kemites, the keepers of the ancient artes, sensed their time coming to an end and merged with the Chosen Bloodlines coming to Sahael. But first, Kaimana and Kanoa sent every Kemite woman to the Neutral Zone to marry and mingle among the Chosen Bloodlines so that Kemettian power would always remain among the Chosen Bloodlines for all time, with full control of Nartica, forcing the Narsans out west."

"I understand clearly now," Lyshyla said.

"I'm glad somebody does," Ozias murmured.

"This land has a complicated history," Chima admitted. "As my adopted father says, anyone who wants history to be simple is looking to have their biases reinforced. I agree with him. What happened here set the stage for how Sahael was infiltrated by Lord Commander Natas and the Narsans as they learned about their tumultuous history and used it to their advantage. The Narsans made their way inside of Sahael and killed the remaining Kemites, enslaving the Chosen Bloodlines."

"This all started with Lord Commander Natas's release," Lyshyla said.

"It would seem so," Oadira said.

Stepping forward, Lyshyla looked at the light in Chima's hand and then at the stone and ice walls around them. "Natas knows all the secrets about the four realms of Aarde. This is why he had the ability to infiltrate Sahael from within. He had access to information that caused all of this."

"Did you know what he planned on doing with the information?" Ozias asked.

"No," Lyshyla said. "You'll remember, the Educators in Timbuktu loved and trusted Natas. His thirst for knowledge was breathtaking."

"Then we must get to Sahael as soon as we can," Oadira said.

"Agreed," Ozias replied. "It looks like there's only one way to go, and that's forward."

"I'll lead the way with my light," Chima said. "Hopefully it will last long enough for us to make it to the other side."

The group followed Chima through the Neutral Zone. Dark shadows danced on the walls as they passed. No sounds could be heard beyond their own footsteps.

Onika walked beside Chima, making eye contact with her. "I heard what you said when we entered this tunnel. What did you mean by, 'Blood will be required to leave this place'?"

"When I cut my palms to open the Kemettian doors, a pact of entry for blood was required," Chima answered. "It allowed knowledge of this place to flow through me for the price of royal blood. My people are a part of the ancient remnants from the beginning that possess, within our bloodline, the same Kemettian power that has been placed inside of the Chosen Bloodlines. Being here comes at a great cost," Chima said.

"What is the cost?" Oadira asked, overhearing their conversation.

"Never mind. It's my problem to worry about, not yours," Chima said.

"Why haven't you written this information down?" Lyshyla asked. "The Educators would love the extra knowledge you provided to me today."

"It's forbidden per the Nairobi laws," Chima replied.

"To what end?" Lyshyla asked.

"To keep an ever-watchful eye on the other side of Aarde and Lord Commander Natas," Chima answered.

"How was Natas released in the first place?" Lyshyla asked. "Natas was cast into the Nothing just outside the three Outer Realms of Darkness rather than being jailed by his parents. His means of escape are unknown to the Educators, but you seem to have knowledge of such things in Carthage."

"We do," Chima replied. "Much of what has been lost is still known here because our people travel the world and have power where most remnants of Sahael do not. Or if they do, choose to remain in hiding like cowards. Natas constructed a replica of Nectanebo's skeleton key, allowing him to leave the Nothing."

"What purpose does Nectanebo's skeleton key serve?" Oadira asked.

Chima shook her head, braids falling over her shoulders. "I don't know. This is why you must get to Sahael to find the answers to the questions you seek."

"We've tried for years to send Educators to the three Outer Realms of Darkness and the Nothing but weren't allowed due to the Nairobi laws," Lyshyla said as she kicked a stone in front of her. "What I do know is that Solomon said Natas roamed Outer Darkness for thousands of years, just wandering and building up all of his hate to unleash on all of Aarde. Lord Commander Natas is using that hate to devise a plan he feels is better than the plan his parents created."

Oadira had long searched for a better understanding of Lord Commander Natas. She had read tomes in Iceoth that whispered of his darkness and learned even more in Timbuktu. Even so, the demon-man remained the ultimate mystery to even the most learned in Aarde.

"Lord Commander Natas didn't like their plan and felt his plan wouldn't lose a single soul compared to his parents," Oadira added. "Whatever his plan is, Natas wanted to save all of his brothers and keep the Andalusian lineage pure."

"I'm not entirely sure how Lord Commander Natas expected to save everyone," Lyshyla said. "He made sure to keep that information from me. I learned also from Solomon that he gained control of the Ennead to work for him, bringing the Outer realms of Darkness into Aarde."

The cavern arched slightly to the left and the group followed Chima and her light steadfastly. The air remained cold and deathly still. Occasionally the sound of dripping water would echo through the passage, but it seemed their voices drowned out all other sound.

Chima continued speaking. "The Ennead are the keepers who were born outside the Outer Realms of Darkness in Aarde and brought inside the realms to watch over the rejected spirits per Ishtar and Obatala orders. They were designated as the gatekeepers to the Realms of Darkness and the Nothing; after the war in Andalusia, the Divines ordered them to maintain an eternal watchful eye over the hosts, ensuring war would never happen in Andalusia again. The Ennead were summoned from the twelve pyramids of Egypt and the lands of Egyptus as spirits watchers."

"I remember reading about this history in Iceoth at the pyramid," Oadira said.

"I do as well," Ozias added.

"Yes, this is well-known throughout Timbuktu among the Educators," Lyshyla agreed.

"This is new to me," Onika replied. "I knew everything about Neir's Realm where I grew up. It's home. But I never studied much about Natas. Many of my peers thought of him as a nightmare being; one who didn't really exist."

"He exists," Oadira spat. "Trust me. I've gazed into his red eyes on several occasions. He is not to be underestimated."

"Onika," Lyshyla said, "Solomon said that three of Natas' four generals were locked up in each of the three realms in Outer Darkness, while Natas himself was sent to the Nothing for all eternity. Natas was given the ability to roam the Nothing, without any learning or understanding. The history of those three realms states their spiritual guardians were promised bodies by Natas, tabernacles of clay that their spirits could dwell within if they helped him get out of the Nothing. They felt rejected by Ishtar and the Divines, so all willingly agreed to help."

Chima nodded in the pale light. "I understand now. It's why they were able to take control and shift their essence from their spiritual form into dead bodies. It's why they're formidable after Lord Commander Natas gained control of the Ennead. He organized them and sent them into every corner of darkness to search for the three spirits of the generals exiled by Ishtar and Obatala. Educator Cantor taught me that Lord Commander Natas learned about them after their betrayal by his father in battle. Natas found a way through Nullify's gate, by opening the iris and passing through Nabopollassar's seal, and Nebuchadnezzar's portal, and then entered Aarde."

"Even with the counterfeit key, how was Natas able to pass through the seal and the gate?" Oadira asked.

"No one knows how he was able to do it," Chima said.

"The only way Lord Commander Natas could have used Nullify's gate and opened Nebuchadnezzar's portal is to have had it opened from the other side," Lyshyla pondered. "What other explanation could there be for Natas being in Sahael and gaining possession of Nectanebo's skeleton key. It's not known how he came to have Nectanebo's skeleton key in his possession. The artifact only allows its owner the ability to pass freely from the Outer Realms of Darkness into the realm of Aarde and back through, not to access the gate or anything else."

"So, all that time he was in Timbuktu, you Educators were teaching Lord Commander Natas how to destroy and enslave Aarde He now has a working knowledge of the estranged tribes with personal and intimate details of their weaknesses are and how to defeat them individually," Chima said, a bite to her words.

"We've already gotten angry with Lyshyla about this, years ago, Chima," Ozias said. "The Educators couldn't have known what evil they were dealing with, or the level of betrayal they faced."

"Still," Chima replied, vein throbbing on her forehead. "Lord Natas will have the upper hand no matter the circumstances, knowing the gifts, powers, and capabilities of each bloodline. The Rysallians were persuaded to live in western Aarde, leading to the Nibiru wall cutting them off from the east, enslaving all of western Aarde."

Lyshyla's face grew red as she seemed to fight back tears of rage. "Western Aarde continues to be enslaved at this moment, and I know the role myself and my class played in it. But our peoples have been divided too long. That's how Natas destroyed the peaceful order in the first place. If all we do is point fingers at each other about who should have known what when, we might as well lie down and let Natas crush our skulls."

"But Lord Commander Natas learned about the Rysallians and their estrangement from the other bloodlines in Timbuktu!" Chima shouted as she stopped walking. Her voice rang through the passage, echoing with anger. Each repeated word seemed to cut to Lyshyla's soul. "Natas used them to help enslave Alkebulan and create a war to justify his invasion into Sahael, to gain possession of Nzingha's obsidian key. Commander Natas wanted to make sure that he couldn't be stopped so he severed the bloodlines, wiping out all of the Kemites in Sahael and enslaving and deporting the four tribes by sending them to different parts of Aarde. They were sent to the mountainous regions in eastern Aarde, the desert sand lands in the northeast, and the ice continent of Iceoth, the final tribe was last seen in Naharis's realm in western Aarde. Lord Commander Natas designed a plan to exterminate them all from Aarde systematically, and it's you and the Educator's fault!"

"It's not," Oadira protested.

"It is!" Chima screamed. "You Educators always think you're better than everyone else. You only share knowledge when it suits you." She looked at Ozias. "Tell me I'm wrong."

Ozias looked down at his feet.

"See?" Chima continued, finger pointing at Lyshyla.

"Educator Cantor always held things back from me. He hoarded knowledge. I hated it! I've known since I was a child that I wasn't as valuable as my 'twin' sister. Once she was gone and we thought she was dead, I believed that would change. Well guess what? It didn't. I would ask Cantor things and he would tell me the knowledge wasn't for me. I wasn't of royal lineage. But I read for myself as much as I could. So now, Educator Lyshyla, you're going to tell me what I want to know right now."

Lyshyla nodded slowly.

"Good! Now, am I right about the four bloodlines being split off to specific sections of Aarde?"

"Yes," Lyshyla confirmed.

"Tell me more. Now."

"A system of eradication was created after the ancient tribes were taken from their homelands," Lyshyla began. "The inhabitants of Alkebulan were enslaved to work their own lands for resources to sustain the west and were then sent to the provinces to be used as labor. After that they were discarded by loading them on boats and sending them to one of the three isolated areas."

"How about we continue walking as we talk," Ozias said, motioning for them to keep going. "That light isn't going to glow forever, and I'd hate to be stuck down here forever in the dark."

"Chima, Lyshyla is telling you the truth about all of this," Oadira said as they resumed their course. "I'm fully aware of the journey she is referencing. I had to sneak onto one of those ships after I led a rebellion on the Lalaurie Estates. After that I found myself in Iceoth. When I made contact with the ocean water for the first time escaping that ship, I set these events in motion, ushering in the Signs of the Times. Over the past thirty years, I have raised my family, and the last two years we've spent performing trials and traveling to Sahael. The currents have brought us closer and closer to our ancestral homeland."

"I understand you insert yourselves into a four-hundred-year-old narrative," Chima said, staring forward into the darkness. "But somehow you just think that getting to Sahael will solve all your problems? You truly have no idea how lucky you are to have made it up to this point; when you arrive, there will be many more obstacles ahead and work to be done. The answers won't just fall into your lap." Chima chuckled, giving a slight scoff and shaking her head. "The events happening around all of you are not by coincidence; they're happening to prevent Lord Commander Natas from finding you and preventing you from getting to Sahael. These events are buying you time. I understand that. I believe that. But soon, the currents will cease to flow all together. What happens to my people then? Will we all suddenly be transported safely to Sahael? No. Will people cease their suffering? No. Will Natas suddenly be overthrown? No. Will the Educators save us? Certainly not.: she paused and took a breath. "Even so, my people will persist until you are safely in Sahael. I'll do what I can as well."

The conversation ended there, with the group walking silently afterward. Oadira understood Chima's frustration. Even when they reached Sahael, more work would be needed to free the people of Aarde. Most believers cheered at the thought of reaching the chosen land, but Chima realized what most others didn't: the world wouldn't magically change when they opened the gates and set foot in Sahael. There would be more building to do, more journeys to take, and more battles to win. More sacrifices would still need to be made. Their journey would just be beginning. The thought made Oadira want to cry.

The light in Chima's hand slowly faded as they continued walking. By the time they saw daylight at the end of the passage, the Illumination Orb barely provided enough glow to navigate by.

They got through the long ice tunnel and entered a clearing of snow where a city of homes stood under a blue sky. The buildings appeared to have been built from Narthax ice in large carved blocks, like crystal. Immediately, the Sec-birds rushed forward and began chewing on whatever grass they could find between the rocks and graveled ground.

"This is the same substance that the pyramid in Iceoth inside of the ice caverns is made from," said Lyshyla as she pointed at the structures.

"These homes and buildings are abandoned," Chima said. "We can stay here and get our bearings before determining where we should go next."

"Have you ever been here before?" Onika asked as he ran his hand along the smooth surface of one of the Nartax blocks.

"No. My father has. He told me about it. Educator Cantor would speak of it sometimes. Many of my people believe this neutral place is cursed."

"We should explore the library," Lyshyla said, pointing to a larger cubed building in the center of the small village with carvings across the top lattice.

"How do you know it's a library?" Ozias asked. "It doesn't look like any of the ones we've encountered before."

"The carvings are the same as the library of Timbuktu," she replied, removing her backpack. "Let's get settled and see if we can find anything to sustain us. The longer our stores of food last, the better."

They stayed in one of the homes in the Neutral Zone while the Sec-birds wandered the area in search of food. Ozias looked around for extra rations as well while Oadira and Onika rested. He discovered snowberries and evidence of rabbits, setting snares before returning to their temporary residence as the temperatures began to drop at sunset.

Lyshyla didn't return until the following morning. She hadn't left the library since their arrival. After a meager breakfast of dried meat and berries, she led the group to the main study chamber in the library center. Light came in through broken windows in the upper ceiling. The air was cold inside, with icicles hanging from the stone tables. The books appeared weathered and tattered after years of exposure from the broken windows.

"I found documents with information on Naharis's realm and the Demirrians," Lyshyla said as she opened a large manuscript with stained yellow pages.

"What about any maps to Sahael?" Onika asked.

"No maps, only clues," Lyshyla answered. "I searched all night. Many of the volumes here are in bad shape, but this one is legible. It seems the Educators that lived here lasted far longer than those in other parts of Aarde. They chronicled new information from after the fall of Sahael, along with writings from Carthaginian sailors bringing news from abroad. Their theories align with much of what we know. Luckily, they have information we don't as well."

"I see you found books on Naharis's realm. What have you read so far?" Chima asked.

"I've read that Nullify's gate is the only one in Naharis's realm in western Aarde that was sealed from both sides," Lyshyla said, running her finger along different passages of text as she spoke. "Natas activated Nebuchadnezzar's portal, and Nabopollassar's turquoise seal by obtaining the materials to create a replica of Nectanebo's skeleton key from inside of the realms of Outer Darkness, as the tales suggest."

"How did Natas acquire the materials to create a replica?" Oadira asked.

"According to this, each Ennead General was persuaded to crush Njiru's onyx rings into little pieces. This was to help Lord Commander Natas construct a replica of Nectanebo's skeleton key from small pieces to control their Ennead Legions. Afterward, the generals gave up their three black keys, enabling Natas to unlock the Outer Realms of Darkness."

"I'm not familiar with these three keys," Chima said.

Lyshyla nodded, flipping a few pages top a drawing of three keys; two black and one pink, "The Jet key, the Black Tourmaline key, and the Apache Tear key allowed him to activate the three realms behind Nullify's gate and Nebuchadnezzar's portal from his side," Lyshyla continued. "This is why Lord Commander Natas had the ability to move freely into Aarde. The three serendibite keys Natas received from the three generals in their jailed realms allowed him and the Ennead commanders to move through Nebuchadnezzar's portal into Naharis's realm. So, from day one, Natas has always been in control of Naharis's realm, giving him the ability to invade the other lands and finally Sahael. That's how Lord Natas gained possession of Nzingha's obsidian key."

"What's so important that would make Natas want to travel back and forth between the realms?" Oadira asked.

"Lord Commander Natas has control over the dead, acquiring the knowledge from the Demirrians," Chima added. "It's why our people are unkind toward Demirrians. Natas used that knowledge to learn about the western and eastern worlds. Educator Cantor would tell my sister that Natas revisited the Outer Realms that were divided into thirds: the Void, the Oblivion, and the Hole.

After the Andalusian war, Ishtar and Obatala sent the Hosts to these three regions, locking them away for eternity, with the generals using their three serendibite keys."

"Those serendibite keys had a one-time use, for the Ennead to lock away the hosts forever," Lyshyla said. "The Ennead were the jailers of these unruly spirits. They had the responsibility to prevent Lord Commander Natas from ever leaving Outer Darkness. The divines commanded that Nzingha and the Kemettian Supreme Leaders Kaimana and Kanoa to create four keys out of Orichalcum. Nzingha created four keys as well: a sapphire key, an emerald key, a turquoise key, and lastly an obsidian key. Supreme leaders Kaimana and Kanoa summoned Nebuchadnezzar to create four rectangular portal doors for the four realms. Kaimana and Kanoa then summoned Nabopolassar to create four seals on Nullify's gate in Naharis's realm and individually in the other three realms."

"Why did Obatala place the keys on Aarde in the first place?" Oadira asked.

"According to these books, three of the four realms are responsible for keeping a watchful eye on Naharis's realm," Lyshyla said.

Chima turned the page on the book in front of Lyshyla. "See? Right here there is a passage that matches one of our histories in Carthage. *'Each of the four realms played a vital role in sealing the gate from this side,'*" she read. "*'The Northern Realm, the Eastern Realm, the Western Realm, and the Southern Realm were each given a key. The Northern Realm was given Nzingah's sapphire key. The Eastern Realm was given Nzingha's emerald key. The Western Realm was given Nzingha's hematite key, and finally the Southern Realm was given Nzingha's turquoise key immediately, and Sahael was given Nzingha's obsidian key that was placed in Sahael.'*"

"Interesting, I'm sure each of the keys served a purpose." Oadira said.

"They did," Chima continued. "Preventing Lord Commander Natas from traveling back through Nullify's gate after using Nectanebo's skeleton key locked him in Aarde. Obatala and Ishtar took every precaution, making sure he could never return to the Outer Realms of Darkness and to keep an ever-watchful eye on him at all times."

"How were they able to accomplish this?" Onika asked.

"Come now, Onika," Lyshyla said, hands on her hips. "I taught you this tale many times when you were a child."

Onika sat down in a stone chair and took a deep breath. "It just goes to show how much I was paying attention. All you ever talk about is history. I'm like my father, a man of action."

"You can't be a man of action without knowledge of history," Ozias said, swatting his son lightly across the shoulder."

"Well, you better listen now," Lyshyla grinned. "Ishtar and Obatala, during the Andalusian war, sent Ra's eye down to Aarde using his abilities to see all and hear all. Keeping an eye on Lord Commander Natas's every move. Lord Natas countered using the eyes of Ne and Ru to help him avoid Ra's eye in Aarde."

"I'm sure Lord Natas was prepared to counter his parents," Ozias said.

"He was," Chima replied. "Sailors often speak of Ne and Ru, under Lord Commander Natas's direction, helping him fight for control of Andalusia during the Andalusian civil wars. As a punishment, they were sent into the depths of eternal darkness for damnation. Ishtar and Obatala took Ne's left eye and Ru's right eye, preventing them from seeing all Aarde and placed them in Sahael, allowing Sahael to see Natas's every move. This allowed Sahael to use this new NeRu eye to monitor the movements of

Natas at all times. They saw everything in the east and everything in the west. Ishtar and Obatala asked Solomon to use Orichalcum clay to mimic NeRu's eye and create a second set of eyes, whose sole purpose and responsibility had been to watch Naharis's realm, the home of the Demir, the race of Black albinos known to some as the Nelio."

"The keys were placed in each of the realms to be a powerful source to help sustain and carry each realm," Lyshyla said, closing the book. "So they could protect and serve Sahael, Egyptus, and Alkebulan at all costs."

"You've talked about Nzingha's four keys for each of the four realms. You've failed to mention what happened to Nzingha's obsidian key. I keep hearing so much about it," Onika said.

"Nzingha's obsidian key was placed in Necrosis's burial chamber in Sahael. It's the key that binds the realms to Sahael," Chima answered.

"What about on the other side of Naharis's realm? Were four seals placed on that side as well?" Lyshyla asked. "Much of what you're telling us is new information even for me. Western Aarde was never my focus."

Chima nodded. "Yes, Lord Commander Natas needs four keys to open the seals from that side to gain reentry into Aarde."

"How?" Lyshyla questioned.

"My people don't know," Chima admitted with a shrug. "The living are forbidden from entering the Outer Realms of Darkness. Even Educator Cantor admitted to not knowing. Of course, much of this he wouldn't tell me directly anyway, but I believe he lacks many of these details as well."

"So, all of this is precautionary to prevent Lord Commander Natas from destroying Aarde as he almost did in Andalusia," Lyshyla said, gazing up at the ceiling.

"That is correct," Chima answered.

Stepping forward, Ozias tapped his finger against the leather book cover. "Lord Commander Natas is looking to finish what he started in Andalusia. He seeks a way to remove the seals that bind Nullify's gate and the portals and seals within it."

"We need to figure out how he's going to do this," Lyshyla said.

"Lord Commander Natas would have to search for the Watchers," replied Chima.

"He'd have to know where they all reside, which Ishtar and Obatala would know since they keep tabs on him," Oadira said. "We've only encountered a couple Watchers during our journey. Not enough to do what we need, or what Natas needs either."

"They dwell within the four realms in eastern Aarde and one in western Aarde," Chima confirmed. "Lord Commander Natas will go to war with them until he's able to get them to give up Nzingha's sapphire, emerald, hematite, and turquoise keys that they were sworn to protect prior to coming down to Aarde. Lord Commander Natas could open up and remove the seals inside and outside of the Nullify's gate, but it would be impossible for him to acquire all four keys."

"You seem certain about that," Lyshyla said with a concerned look on her face.

Chima stepped away from the table and the shaft of sunlight falling on them from above. Her face was suddenly shadowed. "Lord Commander Natas would have to know where each of the realms were located and there is no way he would know where to look. That information is only available in Egyptus where the viziers of Egyptus keep that information that was once kept in the library of Sahael. That is where the Chosen Bloodlines were privy to such information." She looked at Lyshyla. "Am I wrong in this assumption?"

"No." Lyshyla shook her head incredulously. "This is all my fault. I'm the reason why all of this is happening; me and my class."

Oadira watched as Lyshyla's purple tears burned down her cheeks. She tried holding them back but to no avail. She shook her head from side to side, as if to rid her mind of what she'd just discovered. Oadira's face softened with sorrow as she watched Lyshyla's internal pain control her.

"It's okay," Oadira said. She wanted to hug her but decided against it, instead looking directly at Chima with a stone face. "It's imperative that we find out more about these seals; there's no telling if one or all of them are disabled."

"Well, we all know where we need to get to, it can't happen soon enough." Ozias said. "Do we know if Lord Commander Natas had already found the location of the Nzingha's sapphire key in Neir's Realm? Our arrival there led to us restoring life in the realm by obtaining Okavango's heart from Ogum and his wife, releasing Olokun and Yemoja back to the sea. We ensured that the waters never die but remain vibrant and full of life. Could the taking of the ring years before we arrived have led to some of the infected waters?"

"No one ever told us," Lyshyla replied. "Olokun and Yemoja were always open and honest with us while we lived there."

"I've known them my whole life," Onika said, standing up as if to defend the old rulers of Neir's Realm. "They would have told us. I know it."

Oadira took several deep breaths, letting out a heavy sigh. "The best thing we can do now is press on getting to the end gates."

“Good idea. According to this map, the Neutral Zone will take us out of here if we continue traveling west,” Lyshyla said. “There were many riddles about how to get to Sahael from Nartica, but I think I solved them. Once at the ocean, we must follow a specific current that pulls to the west, then the south, then to the northwest, then south again, and then west. It can be discovered, I believe, by following slight algae trails that can only be seen at dusk. If you lose the trail, you’ll get lost in other currents. I think I can navigate from the back of a Sec-bird, if they are strong enough to carry us so great a distance.”

“Let’s rest here tonight and set out in the morning,” Oadira said.

Ozias nodded in agreement. “Onika, you and Chima search the area for as many of those snowberries as you can add to our packs. Who knows what we’ll encounter ahead, and we’ll want as much rations as we can carry. I’ll check the snares and hopefully we’ll have caught a few rabbits. Tomorrow, we set off once again.”

The group traveled through cold and barren lands while the Sec-birds soared overhead. Chima wanted to give the birds as much chance to rest as possible so they could fly on their backs again once they exited the Neutral Zone.

The entourage entered multiple villages over the next few days. Unlike the first grouping of homes they had seen after exiting the passage, these were populated, but sparsely. No matter where they went, the people looked at them warily, choosing to avoid the strangers at all costs. No one would speak to them as they passed through. Oadira watched mothers ushering their children inside at the sight of her family approaching. These people had suffered. They still suffered. Oadira couldn't blame them for their trepidation.

"The people are just looking at us, choosing not to engage," Ozias observed as they left the third village they'd entered since leaving the library.

"They're forbidden from speaking to any of us," Chima said. "They are remnants of the original Ancient Bloodline; this place is so heavily protected that no threats could ever enter…until Natas."

"If some of the original Kemites are down here, why don't we get them to come back to Sahael?" Oadira asked.

"They've chosen neutrality and have fought their war already," Chima said. "That's why this is the Neutral Zone."

By the end of the third day, Oadira and her family came to a collection of towering black rocks that formed a natural maze. At first, they traveled due west, but soon realized the twists and turns had shifted them in all directions.

"We're lost," Ozias breathed as the sun set, throwing them into darkness.

"Where are the Sec-birds?" Onika asked. "We could fly over this area easily with them."

Chima pointed toward the darkening sky. "They're flying somewhere ahead I would assume. At night, they search for grubs and rodents to eat. I bet they're hunting. They'll find us in the morning, I'm sure."

But the Sec-birds didn't return the next morning. Or the morning after that. Or the morning after that, the group simply wandered through the natural maze for days and days trying to find a way out.

Finally, after six days in the maze-like landscape, they crested a hill and could once again see the horizon. Their supply of food had run low, but much to their surprise and joy, the Sec-birds were waiting for them in a field of dry grass that blew in the heavy breeze.

"At least they didn't leave us behind," Onika mumbled.

After two more days of travel, they finally reached the edge of the Neutral Zone, a series of obsidian cliffs similar to what they had seen when entering the Neutral Zone originally. As they drew closer, Oadira could see a set of charcoal doors with silver writing identical to what they had passed through weeks before.

"The opening is up ahead," Chima said.

"Will the ancient Kemites allow us to leave?" Oadira asked, looking back at the closest village, now many miles in the distance.

"Yes, a blood sacrifice is needed to open the doors at this end of the Neutral Zone." Chima replied.

"A blood sacrifice was required to enter. You've already given your blood," Oadira said.

"Ancient blood was required to open the doors to enter, and ancient life will be required to open the doors for you to leave," Chima said. "That's what the writing on the doors says."

The Sec-birds landed beside the family, feet clacking against the stoney ground.

No other sound could be heard as everyone pondered what Chima had just said.

Ancient life? If Oadira understood correctly, and she believed she did, what Chima meant was that one of Oadira's family would need to die in order for them to open the doors.

No mere drop of blood.

A full life.

"This wasn't a part of the agreement. You have no right to put us in this position," Oadira said, looking at her husband and son.

"It's the only way you're able to get to Sahael," Chima said. She looked at Lyshyla. "Am I wrong? Am I misinterpreting?"

The Educator's shoulders slumped. "I believe she is correct. The texts talk about sacrifice, but I've never been focused on Western Aarde. If the door says, 'ancient life,' that's what it means. It makes sense."

"To you, maybe," Onika grumbled.

"I'll do it," Oadira said, stepping forward. "I'll give my life so that all of you may live."

"Then this is all for nothing, and Aarde will fall into ruin. It has to be me," Chima said.

"Why you?" Ozias asked. "You're not of ancient blood."

"She is now," Lyshyla said, shaking her head. "She sacrificed at the entrance, and that sacrifice was accepted by the ancients. She has proven her nobility. The gods will accept her if she chooses to be the life given."

"In order for your family to make it to Sahael, my life is required." Chima said. "I won't let any of you do it. You're too important to the world, to all of Aarde. Like I said when we were in the tunnel, things aren't going to magically change for the better once you enter Sahael. All of you need to be there to fight and defend our people. You are the chosen bloodline. All of this falls on you." She paused and took a breath. "And this falls on me."

The wind blew as everyone stood silent in front of the giant doors. Anger surged in Oadira's veins. How could this beautiful princess who had spent her life always in second place, be asked to give that life just when she had claimed her power and rewrote her very destiny? How could Ishtar and Obatala, the council of gods themselves, be so flippant with noble life?

"What are you saying?" Prince Onika shouted in confusion.

"You know what I am saying," Chima nodded.

"No!" Onika yelled. "This isn't right!"

"Right and wrong are rarely as simple as we make them out to be," Lyshyla whispered.

"Don't give me your Educator garbage!" Onika stomped. "Why should she have to die? Why should any of us have to die?"

Oadira placed her hand on his cheek and smiled. "My son, there are choices in the world we all have to make for the greater good. When that choice is presented before us, we can run away, or we can face it head on. You're going to be a great king one day."

Onika looked up at the sheer cliffs above the doors. "We can fly over! Why do we have to go through the door at all? We have the Sec-birds. They can just take us over the cliffs. That's the answer."

Chima shook her head. "Sec-birds can't soar into the Jetstream. They are too big compared to their wings. While holding us, they would drop. The cliffs are too high, and you can tell by the powerful winds overhead that the gods thought of this potential maneuver. I wish there was another way, Prince Onika, but such sacrifices are part of Aarde itself. There is no way to avoid it."

Onika turned to Oadira, eyes darting in all directions as if looking for a solution in the rocks at their feet. "Okavango's Heart!" he shouted. "It's supposed to get us into Sahael somehow, right? We can use it to get out of the Neutral Zone."

“Okavango’s Heart isn’t some mystical key,” Lyshyla replied.

“I can feel the power ebb and flow through the Heart,” Oadira said, shaking her head. “When in Neir’s Realm it called out to be used as if it knew its purpose. I feel nothing from it here. I’m sorry, Onika, but Okavango’s Heart isn’t going to fix this.”

“There has to be another way!” Onika pleaded.

“Oadira and Ozias,” Chima said as clouds gathered above them. “I have a favor to ask of you that will be difficult. My life must be given for you all to exit the Neutral Zone. It’s the only way these doors can be activated and opened, allowing you to use the Sec-birds to travel the rest of the way to Sahael.”

“We’ll do anything for you,” Oadira said, tears coming to her eyes. “But there has to be another way. Lyshyla, you have to know something that will allow us to---”

“This is the only way,” Lyshyla interrupted, eyes downcast.

“Why?!?” Oadira screamed. The Sec-birds jumped in surprise and stepped away, feathers ruffling in defense.

Oadira couldn’t hide her emotions. Sapphire tears filled her eyes, running down her cheeks. She made eye contact with Chima, who smiled gently.

“I won’t let this happen,” Ozias said.

“It’s okay, Ozias,” Chima said.

“It’s not,” Ozias countered. He paced back and forth as if the movement helped him think.

“You need to have faith,” Chima replied.

“This is your life!” Oadira spat.

“And what nobler way exists for me to give it?” Chima asked. “I could die in battle. I could die sitting idly in my mother’s palace. I could die of starvation. Life is only a moment. The gods have told us that truth many times. This life is like a single breath, and once you let it out, you breathe again on another plane of existence. I don't fear death. I was meant to die in place of my sister if that need ever arose, and when it did, she was the one taken anyway. Now that she is back, I am willing to sacrifice not only for all of you, but for every member of our race who needs to be freed by you. You need my blood, and I give it willingly."

Oadira wiped her tears. Here was true nobility that no bloodline could ever match. Here was choice in its purest form, given freely to save millions of others. Oadira knew a sacrifice was needed, but she didn't want to see anyone sacrifice but her. Why were so many called to give so much? Why couldn't Oadira simply make everything right for everyone? Such a path would be too easy, but still, Oadira longed for easy.

"Oadira, you know better than anyone the importance of fulfilling a destiny," Lyshyla said. "You were chosen before you were formed in the belly of your mother. You were chosen to save Sahael. Chima must die, so that you can live to ensure the success of our mission. I understand how you feel. It's time to be a queen and let Chima die."

"What is the favor you would ask of us, Chima?" Oadira asked slowly.

"Please cut my wrists deeply, that it may be quick and painless," Chima said.

Ozias did as Chima instructed. He conjured a blade with great effort. The blue knife flickered in his hand.

Chima held her wrists out toward Ozias. "You all have work left to do to help Aarde. So, I must give my blood so all may have the future they deserve. I'm happy to give my life. This is all by design; Ishtar's and Obatala's plan for me, I know it."

"There has to be another way," Onika said softly.

"Please forgive me for not telling you, but I had to be sure you would follow through. You've all come this far and must keep pushing. I'll be the final push to help get you there," Chima said, smiling. "I was always meant to die for my sister if needed. Now I will, and for so many others, too. All is well."

"But . . . I just . . . I thought . . ." Onika said.

"Go," Oadira told him. "You must not see this."

Onika turned to leave when his father grabbed his arm. "No, he'll be a king one day and needs to see this. He'll see much worse in the future. He will be forced to make similar decisions and have to live with the consequences."

Onika stood next to Lyshyla as Chima walked slowly to stand between Ozias and Oadira.

"I'll do it," Oadira said, placing her hand on Ozias' wrist.

"Are you sure?" he asked.

"I'm sure."

Oadira blinked her eyes twice, making her irises cerulean. Her tattoos similarly ignited, activating her Orishan gifts. Oadira conjured a dagger. It was far more difficult than it would have been in eastern Aarde, but she held the glowing blade firmly, nonetheless. She stared at the dagger in her hand for nearly a minute.

"It must be done," Chima said once more.

Oadira looked at Ozias, her face drenched and stained with her own tears.

Chima put her hands out in front of her with her wrists facing upward and closed her fists. Walking over to the gate doors, she sat on the edge of a large, white stone slab that rested at the base of the doors. The slab had a circular channel carved at the top that swirled and led to a small reservoir in the center.

Chima lifted her wrists up and exposed them to Oadira. "It is time."

"Your death will not be in vain," Oadira reassured her.

Chima smiled. "It better not be," she said with a hearty laugh.

Oadira placed the cold dagger against the beautiful, brown skin of Chima's wrists and, with one swift motion, sliced them open.

Chima didn't wince as she lay down on the slab, allowing the blood from her wrists to fill the reservoir.

"Oadira, you need to cut my throat so that blood will flow freely into the reservoir," Chima said calmly.

"What?" Oadira was genuinely confused.

"You need to cut my throat," Chima said.

"Wait, no, I . . ." Oadira said as she hesitated, thinking of her mother and the painful memories from when she was a little girl. No daughter should be forced to do such a thing to her mother, and no one should be forced to do such a thing to a noble and brave woman.

"Oadira, we don't have time for objections. Just do it…and be quick about it," Chima said calmly.

Oadira stood behind Chima as she lay on the table. She placed her left hand on her head and gently pushed backward, exposing her neck. Oadira placed her dagger on the soft area of Chima's throat. Her hands started trembling until Nebiriau's bracelet lit up, calming her nerves. She looked down, closing her eyes as tightly as she could as she pressed her knife against Chima's throat.

"Oadira, please," Chima pleaded.

Without hesitation, Oadira gently sliced open Chima's throat with a swipe of her conjured dagger. Quickly the blood trickled from the cut. After a few seconds, Chima started to gurgle and choke. She clasped her neck, trying to do anything to stop her life from ebbing from her body.

Onika closed his eyes and buried his face into his father's shoulder. His father grabbed his head, making him see Chima take her last breaths. Oadira dropped the dagger as it turned into cerulean mist and grabbed Chima's left shoulder and arm. Ozias let go of Onika.

Chima's body convulsed and twitched as the blood from her body moved along the engraved channel, pooling in the reservoir. The slab absorbed the puddle of blood in a matter of seconds. Soon, the ground started to rumble as the gate doors slowly opened. Instead of walking through, Oadira, Ozias, and Onika gathered around Chima's body, dropping to their knees and mourning in silence.

CHAPTER VI

DEAD WATERS

The Neutral Zone

The royal family emerged from the Neutral Zone with Ozias carrying Chima's dead body in his arms. The Sec-birds followed behind them slowly as if in mourning for their trainer and friend. Lyshyla insisted they bury Chima's body outside the doors of the Neutral Zone, so that her body wouldn't be disturbed by the Ennead and the Nethanites. The bodies of the ancients didn't sing, ensuring they wouldn't reveal their locations to the threats in Aarde.

Oadira, Onika, and Lyshyla dug a hole in the ground and laid Chima's body inside it, allowing her to rest for eternity. After covering her corpse with dirt, the doors of the Neutral Zone closed behind them.

"We're at the edge of Nartica Island," Lyshyla said, pointing to the west. The ocean crashed angrily below them as the land dropped off in a series of black cliffs. Gulls squawked in the air above and the cold ocean breeze brought salt to their lips. The storm had arrived with black clouds and lightning over the water. Frigid rain began to fall.

Oadira looked over the Nambissian Sea, using her abilities of interspecies communication to search the water; all she could see was open water and the islands of Britain, Aborigina, and Nier's realm surrounded by Narsan ships.

"I don't see any shelter from the storm," Ozias yelled as a gust of wind pushed roughly against them.

Lyshyla nodded. "Sahael is close by, but we have no way of getting across these waters in this storm. The Sec-birds won't be strong enough to carry us through that tempest."

"There's no way we can reenter the Neutral Zone," Onika said through his tears. "The door is closed to us, limiting our options."

"We press on," Lyshyla said somberly as she tried to deal with Chima's death.

"I need some time to process what just happened," Oadira said solemnly. "Perhaps in the morning the storm will have died down and the birds will be able to fly us across. I haven't felt this way since I was a little girl, when I was forced to cut my mother's own throat. I'm not moving for the rest of the day. Let's find what shelter we can and rest for now."

The storm raged all that night. The family found a small outcropping of rock that protected them from the rain, but it did nothing to stop the harsh winds from buffeting them as they tried to sleep in their blankets. In the morning, little had changed.

"Can we swim across the Nambissian Sea?" Onika asked as he chewed the last of his dried meat rations.

Ozias shook his head. "No, it is too long of a distance to swim. We'd never make it, especially as weak and tired as we all are. Plus, we'll be out of food by the end of the day, with little here in this barren place to replenish us."

They looked around as Chima's Sec-birds rested along the Nartica shore.

"We're not eating them," Oadira said, munching on a piece of stale bread.

"I wasn't going to say that," Onika said with a shrug.

"There used to be a Sec-bird colony in Sahael," Lyshyla said as she too ate what little food remained. "During the fall, the colony was destroyed by the Nitrate bombs the Narsans dropped on the cities and Khartoum Palace. I'd assume they left the area and found a home somewhere else. Sec-birds are prone to always return to their homes in Alkebulan, no matter where they are in Aarde. When we were in Carthage, Chima mentioned to me that these Sec-birds will travel for days to find land that has been colonized by their own."

"We can travel on these birds only for a short time," Ozias said. "We barely made it across the sea from Carthage, let alone a journey of at least twice that far."

Onika stood and tossed his pack next to his father. "I'm going to look around. I can't just sit here."

"It's still raining," Oadira informed, looking at the swollen eyes of her teenage son.

"I'll be fine," he answered as he turned and walked off into the storm.

Of all her boys, Onika had seen the least suffering in his life. His older brothers had been almost as old as he was when they traveled to Neir's realm through the tunnels. They witnessed death and fear, fighting Treep spiders and serving their people with honor. Onika though, had lived in Neir's realm his entire life. Yes, he had been trained like his brothers, but he had never witnessed death firsthand. On a few occasions when an earthquake would strike the land, he had helped the injured to safety, but war and death were a concept more than a reality.

That was all changing now.

Less than an hour later, Onika returned, running through the torrent toward their alcove.

"We may not need to use the Sec-birds at all," he said, dreadlocks dripping with rain. "There's a large ship anchoring in a port a few miles from here to the north. Follow me, I'll show you,"

They followed Onika into the storm, passing an area of tree stumps that stretched to the cliff, as if a forest had once stood here but been cut down some time in the past. The stumps stood like gravestones over a dying land. Oadira soon spotted the docks and the large ship. As they drew closer, Oadira could see the flag of Carthage waving in the rain.

"It's a Carthaginian ship," Ozias said, pointing at the flag.

"How did it get here?" Oadira asked. "The poisoned waters should have torn it to shreds. Travel between Nartica Island and Carthage has been impassable for almost 20 years."

"There's only one way to find out," Lyshyla said as she stepped toward the vessel.

The group made their way to the ship, with the Sec-birds close behind. A group of men loaded crates onto the deck and noticed their approach.

"Who goes there?" one of the sailors shouted through the downpour.

"They have Sec-birds!" another cried, pointing at the large fowls.

"Sec-birds!"

"Who are you?" the first sailor asked again.

"Orishans of Sahael," Oadira called back. "We're in need of travel. Can you help us?"

"That depends on where you're going," a tall man said as he stepped out from behind one of the crates. The man stood about six-feet, nine-inches tall and had bushy black hair, a muscular build, and a braided beard. Lines on his dark weathered face evidenced years in the sun and spray of the sea. He wore a red cloak with a golden broach emblazoned with the symbol of Carthage.

Lyshyla stopped when she saw the man. For a moment Oadira thought her friend and counselor would burst into tears.

"How did you get here?" Lyshyla asked.

The man smiled broadly, showing his ivory teeth. "Lyshyla! By Ishtar!"

"You know each other?" Ozias asked, pulling his cloak closer around him to keep the wind off his face.

Lyshyla stepped forward. "I don't believe it. I thought you were dead when your parents talked about you sailing off."

"What is going on?" Oadira yelled, trying to regain understanding of the situation.

"This," Lyshyla said, arm waving toward the man in the red cape, "is Prince Abdul Chisulo of Carthage."

"How are y'all doing?" Abdul asked with a smile.

"Wait, Chima's adopted brother who sailed off to find Chimalsi?" Onika questioned.

"Lyshyla, it's been a while since the last time you and I worked together," Prince Abdul said, smiling. "Captain Zayn and I were dropping you in Sahael with a six-month-old baby boy, if I remember correctly. It was like 60 years ago, so forgive me---"

"You two know each other?" Oadira asked.

"Let's not discuss that right now," Lyshyla said quickly. "That's a conversation for another day. How did you get here, Abdul?"

The prince nodded. "Why don't we get out of the rain and talk in my quarters. It will be drier and warmer there. Have you eaten? We have plenty of salted fish onboard."

The family followed the prince and his men onto the ship. Through the rain, Oadira saw that the ship had been extensively repaired over time, but appeared to be made of orichalcum, something she had never seen before. The hull glimmered slightly with a metallic sheen, accenting the dents and gouges of what must have seen dangerous voyages on this side of Aarde. The deck featured similar scars, showing the vessel had survived extensive damage in the past, requiring a great deal of repair.

The Prince's cabin was comfortable, with a dining area and large bed next to a row of windows that looked out on the ocean storm. Much of the glass had been similarly patched or replaced as the wood of the ship. Food was brought in by crew members, which was eaten gratefully by the famished family. As they ate, Oadira dreaded telling Abdul about Chima, who had only died the day before. How would he react to hearing he had come so close to seeing his adopted sister again, only to have that opportunity taken away at the last second?

"I was returning to Carthage before the black water forced me to dock," Prince Abdul said after they had eaten their meal. "We would've submerged my submarine ship, but the blackness in the sea prevented us from traveling through the dead sea waters. The windlances on the towers, if not destroyed, would have scuttled my ship as well. It's a chance I could not take until I found my sister, Chimalsi. Eventually there was no way to pass through the water toward Carthage without sinking my vessel and killing all of us."

"But your ship looks to be made of Orichalcum," Ozias mentioned. "Shouldn't it be strong enough to survive the poisoned waters?"

"No, unfortunately. My ship acts like sandpaper against the currents, quickly being torn away. We've suffered a lot of damage over the years simply strafing past the poisoned currents. This ship wouldn't last a day in the toxic ocean. It's also stalled our search for my sister. I'm afraid I'll never find out what happened to her, and I can't get home either. Just my darn luck."

"Princess Chimalsi was found," Lyshyla said. "She was trapped under the Expulsion in obsidian and freed by Onika, who also freed Mami Wata and her daughters."

"That's wonderful!" Abdul said with a large grin. "I knew she was still alive!" He paused and took a deep breath. "I'm filled to the brim. I've hoped for a long time, and to have you say she's okay, that just brings me smiles. Unfortunately, I'm can't return home until something can be done to find a solution to remove the black water from the dead sea. But the fact that you have Sec-birds with you changes everything."

"Why is that?" Ozias asked as he ate the last bite of his salted halibut.

"Because Sec-birds can land in the water safely," Prince Abdul informed. "We discovered it some years ago, but from a distance. The Sec-birds out here aren't trained and fear humans. The birds with you are from my father's collection, correct?"

"Yes," Lyshyla nodded.

"Then we can send someone back to the kingdom with a message!" Abdul grinned. "Heck, we could go two-by-two with one returning each time until we're all home!"

The man's excitement overflowed in his countenance. He'd been trapped here for 20 years and now finally had the chance to go home again. Oadira understood the feeling.

"I have to ask, why are y'all here in the first place? Did y'all travel over or through Nartica?" Prince Abdul asked.

"Yes," Lyshyla said.

"Really? Then how did you gain entry and exit?" Prince Abdul asked. "That land has been cut off for decades since the attack by Natas' forces. There's no way in or out that I know of."

Oadira glanced down at her empty plate. "Chima came with us."

"She did?" Abdul asked. "She was such a quiet girl as a teenager. I'm sure she's amazing now as an adult. Where is she?"

"Chima sacrificed herself, allowing us the ability to leave the Neutral Zone," Oadira said, looking back up. "We buried her body just outside of the exit doors. Your parents are unaware of her death and need to be told as soon as possible."

The prince's excitement faded. He blinked several times.

"She died yesterday?" he asked. "Yesterday?"

"She was incredibly brave," Ozias consoled. "Without her, we would have been trapped, and we needed to get into Nartica to find information on how to navigate to Sahael."

Abdul nodded, a pained look on his face. "I'll have one of my men fly a message to my parents, informing them of Chima's sacrifice. That will provide them and Princess Chimalsi closure."

"And they'll know you're alive," Lyshyla smiled. "That was a relief to learn, and your parents will be overjoyed."

"Now that's settled, I take it you need passage?" Abdul asked. "The west side of Nartica is passable, but the currents are unpredictable to say the least. I can take you to a couple other settlements within a week's sailing, but most of them aren't friendly."

“We’re going to Sahael,” Oadira said.

“Excuse me,” Prince Abdul said.

“You heard her correctly,” Lyshyla said.

“Those are dangerous waters. You’re asking me to enter the nautical trade route,” Prince Abdul said.

“That’s correct,” Lyshyla said.

“You’re asking me to put my crew at risk,” Prince Abdul said. “Plus, no one has made it to the shores of Sahael that I’m aware of for decades. The currents spin ships all over, smashing them into rocks.”

“Yes, but you’ve been there before,” Ozias said. “You told us you took Lyshyla there 60 years ago.”

“I did, but I wasn’t the captain then,” Abdul replied. “I wasn’t 50 years old yet, which is the traditional age a person can become captain in my culture. I didn’t know the secrets of the route, and by the time I came of age, Captain Zayn had been killed in battle and his ship burned. His knowledge of the secret routes was lost.”

“I know the secrets now,” Lyshyla said. “I can guide us.”

Abdul nodded and tapped his finger against his plate. “I can get you as close as I can, but Aarde’s compass shifts to the east, north, west, and south constantly the closer you get to Sahael. They move at a ninety-degree angle. With that said, I don’t know where or how close I can truly get until we leave this side of Aarde. No matter where it is, you’ll have to travel at some point on your own the rest of the way.”

“We’ll take our chances,” Lyshyla said. “We’ll need the Sec-birds, so you’ll have to wait to send your message until they return to you. They’re trained, so hopefully they’ll come back to the ship. All of this is based on faith, so I would ask you to believe for just a little while longer."

"Let's rest for the night," Prince Admiral Abdul said. "I'll make quarters available to all of you and we'll set out in the morning. I'll make sure my men bring the Sec-birds onboard. They are a blessing for all of us, that's dang sure. Until sunrise, rest up, and pray we can make it to the holy land alive and well."

Admiral Abdul ordered his crew to depart and break away from the dock the following morning, traveling the front side of Aarde. Admiral Abdul's ship was the only craft in Aarde made out of Orichalcum, allowing his ship to sail or travel through water or even underwater, when currents weren't present. The ship was 1000 feet long, 460 feet wide; home to 800 Carthinian sailors; and could travel up to 85 knots. It was impressive, and reminded Oadira of what the power of her people could do when not enslaved by cowards and despots.

As far as power was concerned, Oadira, Ozias, and Onika all felt their full strength return during the journey. As they left Western Aarde and drew closer to Sahael, their gifts manifested as strongly as ever. Oadira could once again conjure a sword without thought or effort and felt stronger than she had in months. If they faced battle at any point on their journey, her enemies would die swiftly.

After traveling for three days, the crew notified Lyshyla and the royal family of their whereabouts. Admiral Abdul sailed from the Nambissian Sea into the Nuberrean Sea, sailing past the mountainous lands of Nuberia, outside the obsidian blockade that surrounded Alkebulan.

“This is as close as I can take you before my ship is spotted. If I move any closer, it’ll be difficult to move out of harm’s way if enemies attack,” Prince Abdul said. “I’m going to be honest; I don’t know the way from here either. The ocean mixes with toxic waters all over this section of sea. We don’t have any good options.”

“That’s why you have me,” Lyshyla smiled. She looked out on the horizon. The sun was setting. She waited another twenty minutes before pointing at a pale green glow in the water, hardly noticeable unless someone was looking for it.

“There!” she said. “Follow the algae bloom but go slowly so we don’t lose it. I’ll give directions and coordinates from here on out.”

Prince Abdul’s eyes grew wide. “It seems that the currents are moving for us once more!” Abdul shouted as he grabbed Lyshyla’s slender shoulders, shaking her with excitement. “It’s time for us to leave this place!”

He looked over his ship, gazing at the horizon with a deep look of satisfaction resting on his face. The speed of the ship increased as the wind whipped through Admiral Abdul’s hair and Lyshyla’s long braids. They entered the current and followed it all that night. In the morning, they waited until once again night fell and the algae bloom illuminated their path.

“The currents are making us move faster through the waters at one hundred and twenty knots,” Admiral Abdul said that evening as he entered his quarters for the evening meal with his guests. “But as I feared, toxic waters have started to become too plentiful. If it continues, we won’t be able to go much farther once the sun rises.”

“That means we’ll be at our drop-off point soon. Be ready,” Lyshyla said as she took a bite of dried fruit.

As the sun rose the following morning it became obvious the toxic waters had taken over despite the algae bloom's path. Black waves crashed against the hull with a scraping sound that sent chills up Oadira's spine.

The ship could go no farther.

They spent the next few minutes getting ready to leave Admiral Abdul's ship.

"It is time for y'all to make your jump off my ship. We need to turn back within the hour, otherwise the ship could come away with heavy damage. We're moving at a fast pace. Y'all need to use your Sec-birds to make it the rest of the way," Abdul said, pointing toward the west.

With a high-pitched whistle from Oadira, all the Sec-birds ran across the deck.

"Climb on your birds!" Oadira ordered. The family each picked a fowl and climbed on.

Before mounting her Sec-bird, Lyshyla patted the feathers of the bird that had been Chima's mount.

"Prince Admiral Abdul," she said. "We no longer have need of the Sec-bird that Chima rode to Nartica. I offer it to you to send your message to your parents. Hopefully it will be the means of you returning to your country once again."

"Thank you, Lyshyla," Abdul said, smiling. "you're a darn fine woman."

"Enough talking!" Oadira shouted. "Get on your bird, Lyshyla, and let's take off. On three! One! Two! Three!"

All four Sec-birds flapped their wings, and with great effort, took to the skies with their passengers. The birds and their travel companions made their way east up the lower passage as Abdul's ship grew smaller and smaller in the distance until it completely vanished from sight.

They flew for several hours as far as they could, until the Sec-bird's wings flapped more and more slowly. They lowered close to the water, panting. In the distance, Oadira made out a landmass. It was an island but would give the birds a chance to walk around and forage for food.

"The birds can no longer fly. Let's allow them time to rest on that island ahead," Oadira said.

The birds flew downward, landing on dark and dreary terrain. As the family dismounted, the Sec-birds quickly flew away.

"Where are they going?" Onika asked as the Sec-birds took to the sky and flew away as if they were being hunted by a predator.

"Damn it!" Ozias shouted. "Now what do we do?"

Lyshyla looked around with a frown on her face. The area was desolate and barren. Gray soil stretched to the horizon as if the land was covered in ash. Skeletons poked here and there from the dirt with their dead grins.

"What is this place?" Oadira asked as she knelt down and brushed ash from a skull.

"It stinks," Onika said. He waved his hand in front of his nose to dispel the stench.

"I'm not sure which Island this is," Lysha answered. "I have theories, but let's move inland and see if we can find anything to help us."

"Why did the birds leave?" Onika asked.

"I don't know," Lyshyla replied. "But it doesn't bode well for us, or the spirit on this island. Be wary."

The reek of death got stronger as they moved closer inland.

No life could be seen for miles in any direction. Remnants of burned Marula Trees stuck from the ground like clawing fingers. The smell of the land possessed a strong, moldy odor that caused them all to place their hands over their noses until they grew accustomed to the pungent odor.

"Njal Island was declared dead after the invasion of Sahael and the destruction of Khartoum Palace," Lyshyla said as they walked through the ruins of a small village. "That's where I think we are. The Narsans bombed the island on their way out of Sahael, making sure there were no survivors hiding out on the island."

"These Narsans don't mess around," Onika said.

"The Narsans left no stone unturned. They wanted to destroy anything that could've been a possible salvation for Sahael," Lyshyla answered. Sadness spread across her face. "Many years ago, when the ancient families were enslaved, a poisonous liquid appeared in the waters, killing anything it came into contact with much like the waters of Sahael."

"How did all of this poison appear from out of nowhere?" Oadira asked.

"The poisonous water appeared because Sahael had been given a failsafe by Ishtar and Obatala, that if the land ever fell for invaders, it would become uninhabitable until the return of the chosen bloodline. Right now, the air, water, and land are poisoned. Water can also be made acidic when large numbers of Orishan bodies are cast into the ocean. The Narsans did some of it themselves without meaning to when they slaughtered women and children before throwing them to the sea."

"I remember you teaching me about this as a kid," Onika said.

"You're still a kid," Ozias smiled.

"Anyway," Onika continued, a look of annoyance on his

face. "If there's nothing in Sahael, if the whole place is dead, what are we going to do? There won't be anything to eat. And can we even breathe the air?"

"Your powers will be completely restored when you arrive in the homeland," Lyshyla said as she accidently stepped on a skeleton and crunched through its chest cavity. "Your protective skins will form, allowing you to breathe."

"And what about you?" Onika asked.

Oadira smiled. Her son still had so much to learn about Lyshyla. Oadira herself still had so much to learn about the woman and knew Lyshyla could take care of herself.

"I'll be fine," Lyshyla replied. "You don't need to worry about me. As for everything else, the gods have prepared a way. I don't know what it is yet, but like everything else on our journey, it will manifest itself in time."

A warm feeling touched Oadira's chest and she knew Okavango's Heart reacted to the truth of Lyshyla's words.

They continued walking through the scarred land, finding more ruins and skeletons as they went. Onika's pace slowed somewhat, as if he carried the weight of the dead on his shoulders.

"Why would they do this?" he mumbled.

"In many ways, these are the lucky ones," Lyshyla replied, waving her hand toward the bones all around them.

"Why is that?" Onika asked.

"Many of the Orishans were enslaved, as you know," she replied. "Their lot was more terrible. Ask your mother about the slave ships. She was on them. Many of our people jumped overboard. They felt suicide was better than being chained. Some of them made it to this island. Little did they know, they were followed and hunted down by General Commander Norg and his

Narsan SS. They wiped out men, women, and children."

"A lot of unfortunate events took place around Sahael with the death of the four bloodlines," Oadira pointed out.

Lyshyla took a deep breath and looked to the sky. "The same cataclysmic event happened with the other islands in Sahael, with many of the Yorubans dying at the hands of Norg and his Narsan SS. The Yoruba attempted to run away from Khartoum Palace, but many were captured and placed on massive slave ships all because they possessed emerald eyes."

Onika's eyes shifted to Lyshyla's. He seemed to study her closely.

"If the Orishan bodies made the waters acidic like you said, what effect did the Yoruban bodies have on the grounds of Sahael?" Oadira asked.

"When the Yorubans were killed by their obsidian weapons, it created a deadly reaction when their bodies hit the ground. It led to another fatal event that took place. Their red blood and their emerald souls started interacting with the land as their blood soaked the Sahaelian ground and spread throughout Sahael," Lyshyla said.

Onika pulled on Lyshyla's clothing to get her attention. Lyshyla. "What effect did the bodies have on the land?" he asked.

"When the obsidian interacted with the Yoruban body upon death, the bodies instantly became poisonous to the land, turning it into ash and killing all of the animals, insects, and reptiles that fed upon it," Lyshyla answered. "The third bloodline in Sahael were the Hausans, who attempted to fly away but were taken out by Lord Commander Natas's Netson speeders and windlances. The Narsans used obsidian weaponry—all kinds of strange cannons and unknown weaponry. They even used arrows, crossbows, and lances to fire at the skies of Sahael right above Khartoum Palace.

They did this with horrific ease, shooting the Hausans out of the sky. As they were being shot down, their bodies remained in the Sahaelian skies, suspended in the air. As this happened, the third of the four catastrophic events took place. The Hausan bodies that were suspended in the Sahaelian air started to decompose, causing the air to become acidic. This prevented General Norg and the Narsan SS from taking control of Sahael, thus saving it from occupation.

"The last of the four bloodlines, the Demir, were hung from every Marula Tree in Sahael, until their necks snapped, reacting with the ground to make it poisonous to step on, infecting and killing anyone who touched Sahaelian land."

"Based on what you've said, it seems the deaths of the four bloodlines triggered the safety mechanism that saved Sahael," Oadira said.

"Saved Sahael?" Onika chuckled without humor. He kicked a skull that went rolling into the ash with a puff of dust behind. "Sounds like it destroyed Sahael. What a pointless thing. All those plants and animals dead, and for what? To keep Natas out? This whole thing is pointless."

"It's not pointless," Ozias said. He glanced at Oadira for help with their son.

Lyshyla kept talking as if unaware Onika had spoken. "Many Sahaelians that were killed, and their bodies morphed into a dangerous substance, creating poisonous, acidic gasses, liquids, clouds, and dirt that made Sahael uninhabitable. It forced anyone and everything out of Sahael. As the acidic clouds lowered from the sky, it triggered everything inside of Sahael simultaneously,"

Lyshyla stopped and closed her eyes. She kneeled to the ground and picked up a handful of ash. "This island is our way back into Sahael. This destruction is too focused. Natas knew something about this island. It's the only explanation for it being so completely decimated. Lord Commander Natas ordered the Narsan airships to destroy this place, knowing this island had a direct correlation to the four families of Sahael. I have a theory. Let's continue up the hills to the north and see what we can see from up there.

They crested the hills just as the sun set. There below them in a valley, catching the last rays of day, was a small lake surrounded by blue lotus flowers. The flowers had faded substantially and appeared to be dying, but they were still alive among all the ruin; the only life they had seen that day. The pond itself seemed as dead as the land surrounding it.

"Look at that," Ozias smiled. "There is some life here after all."

"Let's get a close look," Lyshyla ordered.

As they approached the pond, a warm feeling filled Oadira, as if Okavango's Heart began to sing in her mind.

"Mother!" Onika shouted. "The necklace around your neck is lighting it up, as are your eyes and tattoos."

"Okavango's Heart is glowing brightly around you the closer you get to the flowers and the pond," Ozias said.

Lyshyla gasped softly. "The water is glowing too. Look!"

Indeed, the pond itself lit up from far beneath the surface. They all rushed to the banks to gaze into the dark water.

"There are seven symbols at the bottom of the pond, the seven Alkebulan powers," Lyshyla breathed. "Do you see them through the brackish mire? The pond is several hundred feet deep,"

Oadira stared at the light, blinking her eyes to activate her dark sight. As she focused, the outlines of symbols became clearer.

"There's also a large kyanite stone at the bottom of the pond floor losing its color," Lyshyla continued. "The kyanite stone has an empty slot in it."

"I don't see the slot," Onika said.

"You need to know what to look for," Lyshyla replied.

Okavango's Heart continued to blaze bright against Oadira's chest. There was a connection here she couldn't deny. The Heart wanted to go into the water. She knew it.

Without a word, Oadira dove into the water and swam to the bottom of the pond as fast as she could. She held her breath, afraid the poisoned water would choke her lungs. Seeing the empty slot on the kyanite stone pulsating, Oadira took Okavango's Heart from around her neck. It was too big for the slot in the stone, but she noticed one of the nine pieces of the heart glowing more brightly than the others. With a bit of force, she pulled the sliver of sapphire from the heart and placed it in the empty slot.

Instantly the water rushed around her as if being drained. A hidden door opened in front of her, pulling the water from the pond. Oadira swam against the current until no water remained in the little pool.

"There's a Nibiru door opening forcing the water to recede," Lyshyla shouted from the banks.

Ozias, Onika, and Lyshyla stepped into the mud and slowly slipped and slid to the bottom of the now waterless depression.

"Where does that door go?" Onika questioned, wiping mud from his hands on his traveling robes.

"There's a Nibiru tunnel inside of this pond that should take us through Dead Water Pass," Lyshyla said, practically shaking with joy. "It is as we were promised. The gods smile on our journey. The Sec-birds may have feared this place, but Ishtar has supplied another way to get to Sahael. Let's go!"

Okavango's Heart led the way through the dark tunnel as it never stopped glowing. Oadira thus took the lead, holding the remaining eight stones aloft to give them as much illumination as possible. The tunnel walls were smooth and rounded, as if ancient machines had carved the passage.

"I hate tunnels," Onika snapped. "It seems like all we do is walk through tunnels underground. Why couldn't the gods have made all of this easier?"

"Life isn't easy, Son," Ozias replied. "Perhaps yours has been…growing up safe in Neir's Realm. But for most people, it is difficulty and pain. You need to learn this before you become ruler of anything bigger than your own mind. The ancients thought of everything when they put safeguards in place to ensure their people can always get out of harm's way."

"There's nothing to worry about in this tunnel," Lyshyla said, walking close to Oadira. "It was used as a Sahaelian secret that has been in the four families for many years. After the fall of Sahael, it was this tunnel that your mother and father were supposed to use but chose not to because they wanted to defend Sahael and its cities. It was originally a part of the plan to have the royal families travel through this tunnel safely to get to the Neutral Zone until it was time to return to Sahael. Admiral Abdul was to meet them here and transport them to Nartica Island. Unfortunately, no one ever thought Sahael could fall. Pride is a dangerous thing, and it certainly ensured our land succumbed to its enemies. There was too much secrecy as well. The four houses in Sahael kept information from the Sahaelian Congress, for fear of having that knowledge fall into the wrong hands."

“Maybe you Educators should have had that same policy,” Ozias mused. “Then Natas wouldn’t have known every way to destroy the royal families.”

Lyshyla shook her head. “No matter what you think of the Educators, Ozias, secrecy is never good. Never.”

“That is something that we can’t control once Sahael is reestablished,” Oadira said, wanting to cut off any argument that might form from this line of talk. “We never know who our true enemies are until they commit the acts that make them our enemies.”

After several hours, the tunnel sloped steadily downward until they came to water. The light reflected off the surface, showing that the tunnel became completely flooded less than a hundred yards in front of them.

“Looks like this was prepared for the Orishans,” Lyshyla said. “We’ll be swimming from here. There is an underwater cavern somewhere ahead where we’ll have to travel on the leatherback sea turtles to cross Dead Water Pass. We’re not going to have much time. The barriers keeping the water out of this cavern are weakening. Using the leatherbacks to travel through the permeable barrier will allow us to travel on top and across the water cliffs. Keep in mind, this is a place where the water has a strong vertical density as it falls off from the water cliffs. It will be hard to know which way is up and which down once you are submerged. Hold tight to your packs and supplies. We can’t afford to lose what food and water we have left. There won’t be any more to find on our journey that I know of. We will trust in the gods. Follow me.”

They abandoned their backpacks and swam through the dark water for another hour. Even with their skin evolved to brave the deepest ocean, the water still felt brutally cold against Oadira’s body. She sensed Onika’s frustration as they traversed the tunnel.

He continually looked at Lyshyla, face angry and resentful.

She understood.

Lyshyla always knew more than she let on. Oadira had gotten used to it over the last 30 years, but Onika was just now understanding the true annoyance of being given information only when it was needed. The longer they traveled together, the more Oadira understood why her ancestors preferred the Educators to stay in Timbuktu as opposed to being at court all the time.

They broke the surface in a dark cavern with tall ceilings. Shafts of daylight shot through unseen openings here and there overhead. To their left spread a large sand beach that was covered, as Lyshyla had suggested, with immense sea turtles, some ten feet from snout to tail, broad shells glimmering in the patchy sunlight.

"I'll help round up leatherbacks," Oadira said as she swam toward the beach. "There are hundreds of them that live in this cavern. Then we can continue onward to Sahael."

"I'll look for the Nibiru tunnel exit that takes us to Leatherback Island," Lyshyla said. "If we continue to follow the Nibiru tunnel, it should lead us through the waters to a small island called Leatherback Island; it can be our launching point to travel across Dead Water Pass."

"Why is it called 'Dead Water Pass?'" Onika asked, spitting water from his mouth as he floated. "Didn't the water become dead after the fall of Sahael?"

"Names change," Lyshyla called back as she swam away. "Or maybe it was called that from the beginning because of its dangers. Don't let your pride convince you that you know everything, little Prince." She swam below the surface and disappeared.

"At least I'd tell people what they were going to face before it was staring at them ready to attack," Onika mumbled.

"Onika!" Ozias shouted. "Help us get the damn turtles and stop whining!"

"Yes, Father."

An hour later, Lyshyla returned, swimming up to the beach. She rang the water from her hair and sat next to Oadira, breathing heavily.

"I swam back as fast as I could. I found the tunnel. The current is swift and dangerous, so it's a good thing we have the turtles."

"Has traveling across Dead Water Pass ever been done?" Oadira asked as one of the leatherbacks nudged her shoulder. "How certain are you that we'll make it across the treacherous waters safely?"

Lyshyla breathed deeply several times before answering. "The stratification of the water can change its salinity and temperature, or both, at a moment's notice. The water can get so hot that it can burn the skin right off your body directly to the bone like a hot knife through butter. It can also get cold. If you put your finger in, it would be excruciating, like hitting rocks. I assure you; we'll all be safe as long as we stay on the leatherbacks. They travel up and down Dead Water Pass to mate, leaving their nests to multiply and replenish."

"They'll keep us safe," Ozias said softly to Onika.

"Let's go," Oadira ordered. Lyshyla nodded, fatigued, but Oadira knew her friend would never be the reason they were slowed down, no matter how tired they were.

After swimming underwater with their turtles beside them, they emerged in the open sea. Waves crashed against them and bobbed them up and down in the afternoon sun. It was good to feel light on her face again, and Oadira wanted nothing more than to rest and relax on a warm sand beach, but they were so close. Rest would come later…she hoped.

"Climb on your leatherbacks," Lyshyla cried. "The Dead Water is only a mile ahead."

The shells of the sea turtles were slick but contoured enough to grab hold. They all climbed on, and Lyshyla patted the head of the lead animal and whispered to it. The turtle bellowed and set off toward the west, followed by its companions. The leatherbacks swam swiftly, keeping their passengers from touching the water.

Dead Water Pass was a series of intertwining rivers that crossed into one another, known to shred the skin off anyone who fell into their currents. They traveled safely through the Dead Water on top of the leatherback turtles. The sun burned hot as the day progressed. Eventually the current sped up, pulling them from the west to the south. Soon a rush of sound grew louder and louder, like a waterfall pounding rocks.

"The sinkhole!" Lyshyla cried.

A whirlpool opened before their eyes, spiraling to the depths. The turtles tried to swim away, but the flow was far too powerful.

"My empress!" Lyshyla yelled over the crushing sound. "Throw a piece of Okavango's heart inside of the sinkhole!"

Oadira took a second blue shard from Okavango's heart and threw the Neolithic piece into the whirlpool. Immediately, the Dead Waters calmed, allowing the leatherbacks to swim smoothly once again.

"Allow the leatherbacks to guide us," Lyshyla said to everyone as the sea calmed and the currents returned to their westerly flow.

As the sun drew toward the horizon, Oadira caught her first glimpse of land.

Could it be Sahael? After all these decades, all of her adult life, was she finally looking at the shores of her homeland?

"Is that Sahael?" Onika asked.

"It's the barrier!" Lyshyla called from the front turtle. "The currents lead to the door. Be ready!"

The leatherbacks carried Oadira, Ozias, Onika, and Lyshyla to the front of the Orishan gates; large rocky cliffs of jagged gray granite with natural spikes along the shore. Twin Orichalcum doors, similar in design and apparent function as the other doors they had passed through on their journey, stood before them, a large letter 'O' emblazoned on the front.

Oadira looked up at the Orishan gates and immediately saw an empty slot emanating cerulean just like her eyes and tattoos.

The turtles swam up to the rocky shore before the gates, and the family climbed off their backs. The tiny beach in front of the doors was made of black pebbles, with the waves crashing right up against the gates themselves. Oadira assumed that during high tide, the bottom of the doors would be completely submerged.

"Oadira, there's another empty slot," Lyshyla said, pointing at the gate. "Please remove a third piece of the Okavango's heart and place it inside of the slot."

Oadira observed the Orishan gate, hesitating to insert the third piece as she was overcome with a wide range of emotions.

"This is the only way we are going to get to Sahael from this side of Aarde," Lyshyla said. "These are the Orishan Gates."

"I'm wondering why these doors are closed in the first place," Oadira said, inspecting them closely. "No one was left behind to close them after Natas attacked."

"After the fall of Sahael and the four bloodlines were removed, the gates closed automatically to prevent the poisonous and acidic waters from spreading throughout Aarde and killing life on every continent," Lyshyla answered. "Once these doors open, we'll not have much time before the acid spreads and kills all sea life, nullifying the effects of Nier's realm."

"I'm not sure if it's worth putting Aarde in extreme danger. If we open these gates, we'd be putting the knife to everyone's throat," Ozias said.

Lyshyla shook her head. "It matters not. You'll have an opportunity to save every body of water in Aarde while getting your home in order. Nothing survives unless Sahael survives. Now, before we enter, know that As soon as we pass beyond these doors, I'm not sure of what to expect. Over fifty million slaves died in chains traveling through the Middle Passage. The waters here are unforgiving. Before ships could start the Nautical Trade, they had to be a certain weight, ensuring they'd have enough food to feed the enslaved. If they didn't have enough food, they'd chain slaves to a boulder and throw them overboard, to lessen their weight."

"That is downright awful." Oadira said.

"Colonizers are pre-dispositioned to always do acts of evil. White Darkness has crept into their hearts, making it easy for them to justify their actions," Ozias said. His eyes were narrow with disgust.

"The Middle Passage is where most of the death in Sahael took place for the Orishans and the Chosen Bloodlines. It was utter destruction and chaos," Lyshyla explained. "Be prepared. Make sure the turtles remain close so they can lead us through the water toward the mainland. And activate your Orishan abilities now so your skin can become hard and durable. You'll need to sustain the arte for as long as you can. I know you will get tired, but you cannot lapse in keeping your body protected. The air itself will kill you within moments."

Onika stepped forward and touched the doors as a wave crashed behind them. "What about you, Educator Lyshyla? You don't have our same gifts since you are not of the Royal Bloodline of the Orishans. How will you survive?"

A cold look passed across Lyshyla's face. Oadira wanted to chide Onika for pushing Lyshyla at such a time, but she understood his resentment toward the woman. It took Oadira years to understand the Educator's ways. And maybe it was good for Lyshyla to understand the impatience of youth, and how secrets can taint a relationship. Onika had lost trust in Lyshyla, that much was obvious, and it had more to do with her actions than it did with his. He had followed loyally and bravely despite his few complaints. He was only 17 after all. If Lyshyla wanted him to trust her council, she would need to understand his irritations and respond accordingly.

"I'll be fine," Lyshyla said, lips barely moving.

"And I suppose we'll have to wait to see how," Onika replied, equally as serious.

Ozias pulled his son back. "Enough! We're on the shores of our damn homeland. Both of you need to figure out how to communicate or I swear to Ishtar you can stay here on the other side of the gates." He looked at Oadira. "Let's get this over with."

Oadira placed the piece in the slot below the 'O.' Immediately the symbol lit up to match Oadira's cerulean eyes and tattoos.

The doors creaked and slowly swung open. Acidic water suddenly poured out, gray and steaming. The family tried to dodge the deluge but had nowhere to go beyond the small beach. The water stung their skin as it flowed into the ocean.

"Run and swim as best you can!" Lyshyla shouted as she darted forward. Oadira and the others followed, wading through the torrent with the turtles close behind. As soon as they passed through, the doors shut behind them, holding back any more poison water from infecting the seas beyond.

On the other side of the gate the sky was milky-white with mist. They floated in the water now, and Oadira felt the acidic liquid trying to burn through her Orishan protections. Concentrating on her body to keep her skin and throat fully encrusted and hard would take a great deal of effort, but she could feel what would happen if any of them faltered. Death would be immediate.

Nothing could be seen beyond the fog. The mist itself was thick, smelling of chemicals and unnatural flavors as she breathed.

"Concentrate on your protections," Lyshyla repeated. She climbed onto the back of the nearest turtle. "Ride the leatherbacks once more. I don't know how long they can survive here, but we need them as long as they live."

The leatherbacks took the group through the waters and the mist, following a weak current that Oadira assumed was taking them to the west. She could see nothing through the vapor.

Darkness fell and the turtles stopped at an outcropping of stone to rest. There was little space available, but Oadira and her family huddled for the night while acidic waves crashed against them. The turtles wheezed and coughed, obviously falling victim to the poisons despite their hardy constitution. No one slept, as the thought of losing concentration and removing their protective skins brought thoughts of suffocation and death.

Lyshyla dozed, somehow impervious to the environment

without needing any magics or hidden artes they could see. Onika would glance at her from time to time as she slept, eyes hard, face like stone.

The mist grew brighter around them and Oadira assumed the sun had risen, though she couldn't see exactly where it was in the sky. They were all wet, tired, and uncomfortable. With their powers returned though, Oadira knew they could continue the journey without food or rest for several more days if needed.

"The leatherbacks are starting to weaken," Lyshyla said as she stared into the fog. "The acid took a heavy toll on them yesterday. I believe they will have strength enough to reach the forest shores of Yaterga and Kurukeia."

"What happens to the sea turtles once we reach shore?" Omika asked, patting the shell of his choking companion.

"They die having given great service," Lyshyla said, though emotion pulled at her face despite the harsh truth. "We need to travel through Yaterga Forest. You'll need to continue using your Orishan abilities to move through the acidic clouds that have fallen upon the forests. Avoiding the Sahaelian bears is a must."

"Wait, there are bears still alive in Sahael?" Ozias asked. "How is that possible?"

"They survive the same way I do," Lyshyla said as she nudged her weak leatherback off the rock and into the water. "They know how."

After less than two hours of travel, land appeared through the fog. The contaminated water crashed in waves against the shore. Dead trees stood like arthritic hands above them, dark and menacing. The turtles lay in the sand as they landed, barely breathing.

"Thank you," Oadira whispered to her leatherback,

touching its head. "Your sacrifice will mean the lives of millions, my ancient friend. May you find swift and painless passage to the chosen realms of peace."

Oadira stood and looked out on the mist-covered land.

This was Alkebulan.

For 30 years she had an image of this place in her head, one that was green and verdant, inviting to her and all people. What she saw was a scar on the face of Aarde that would kill anyone that set foot here. She and her family needed to concentrate continuously in order to protect themselves from instant death.

How could this land be redeemed?

It suddenly felt more impossible than anything she had ever faced. Here was the ultimate challenge, and though she trusted the gods, her faith faltered in the shadow of the dead trees and still air.

They left the beach and walked into the desiccated forest.

"The acidic air is making it difficult to travel," Onika said as he coughed. "It's so thick I can't even see my hands out in front of me. I see nothing alive in this forest—birds, foxes, and rodents are all dead, even the insects."

Twigs snapped under Lyshyla's feet as she led the way. "The acidic skies are a safety mechanism to protect the remnants of the dead and the remaining bones of the Ancient Bloodlines. When the threshold of death has been reached, they are activated to protect and preserve. It has been this way for over four hundred years, a mechanism that will be lifted when Aarde is in balance. We have a long way to go, so let's keep moving."

CHAPTER VII

THE DEATH AND LIFE OF SAHAEL

The Continent of Alkebulan

The group traveled all that week through the desolation, passing ruined cities and towns on their way, trekking over hills and valleys, finding no life whatsoever. After the first three days they had to stop and rest, finding a cave that ran deep into a mountain where the air inside was breathable. They slept for an entire day. They hadn't eaten anything since arriving in Alkebulan. The hunger began to pull at Oadira's stomach. She could tell Onika felt the same way, but to his credit, the young man pushed forward silently, conserving what strength he could.

By the seventh day, their supplies of food and water were completely gone. They had conserved as best they could, but now they would be hungry and thirsty moving forward through the toxic air. Oadira's throat scratched as she swallowed, her tongue growing thick in her mouth. They stumbled along following Lyshyla, placing one foot in front of the other.

Finally, after the eighth day of smoke and rotten

landscapes, they reached Sahael's crater; the natural boundary in the center of Alkebulan. Steep bluffs rose over a round depression several miles wide where the meteor had hit in ages past, bringing the Kemites to Aarde in the first place. Oadira had longed to see the crater from the upper rim, but now wanted only to reach some safe place where she, her husband and son, could rest, drink, and eat.

"Yaterga Forest ends at the crater walls that surround all of Sahael. Short-haired bears live inside caves on both sides of the Sahaelain gate. We need to avoid them at all costs. They are dangerous and wild," Lyshyla said.

"So, no finding respite in a cave like last time," Ozias nodded. "Where to from here?"

Lyshyla pointed to the south along the crater's base. "To find the great Sahaelian Gate that will allow entrance to Sahael itself. The crater acts as the final protective wall to the land

They walked along the outer base of the crater for another hour, following Lyshyla as she searched through the fog for the great Sahaelian Gate. Then, through the mist, Oadira saw it. Black doors of orichalcum standing 100 feet tall, carved with intricate designs for each of the four bloodlines. The Orishan symbol was on top, while the Yoruban and Hausan were below, with the Demirrian on the bottom.

Ozias pointed to the Orishan symbol. "Above the Orishan crest there's an empty slot like what we saw on the gates leading to Alkebulan. I bet another piece of Okavango's Heart goes in there to open the gates."

A set of stairs had been cut into the rock on the right side of the gate, allowing Oadira to climb and reach the empty slot. She inserted the fourth piece of Okavango's heart. The Orishan symbol glowed, but the door didn't open. Instead, two stone tablets raised on either side of the gate and water began pouring out in a torrent.

Onika cried out in surprise. Instead of pooling at the base of the gate though, the water began swirling as if pulled into the ground like a large whirlpool.

"What is that?" Ozias shouted over the rush of water.

"The main gate won't open apparently without the other four bloodlines placing their relic in the sacrificial altar cove." Lyshyla said. "This must be a way in that only Orishans can use."

"Are you sure?" Oadira asked as she leaped down the rocky stairs.

"Honestly, this is new to me as well," Lyshyla admitted. "I've never entered Sahael this way."

"Then how do we know it's not a trap?" Onika asked as water splashed against his ankles.

Oadira waded through the water, feeling the pull toward the whirlpool. She reached her son and placed her hand on his shoulder.

"Faith is how we know it's not a trap," she said, nodding her head.

"It seems we need to get wet," Ozias said.

Lyshyla stepped into the water and looked back at what remained of the royal family. "I know there's a second set of gates deep below the Middle Passage waters. This must be what leads to it for the Orishan Bloodline. They're the Sahaedron Gates. We need to enter the whirlpool."

"We're getting closer, and this is our only option. Let's all jump and hope for the best," Oadira said as she and the others jumped into the whirlpool.

The water was cold and contained the same carcinogens as the ocean waters around Alkebulan. Breathing it in burned slightly, but Oadira soon grew accustomed to the sting.

The whirlpool took them deep down into the depths of the Middle Passage; caves and tunnels built over centuries. Even with their Orishan sight, the darkness was all encompassing. They were pulled along for several minutes in complete blackness, praying the current would lead them where they needed to go.

Suddenly a pale glow illuminated ahead, blue and peaceful. The Sahaedron gates had opened entirely, their carvings and symbols shining in the dark like a beacon. The current pulled them through and shifted upward. In a geyser-like explosion, the water shot into the air, spitting Oadira and her family into a river that flowed under gray skies and the poisoned air of Alkebulan.

"The water is dark and will be difficult to navigate and swim through due to the number of dead bodies and skeletons everywhere that have left a dark-blue residue in the water," Lyshyla said as she swam.

"The sooner these waters are cleaned up, the better it will be for Sahael, Alkebulan, and Aarde," Oadira said.

Ozias swam over, holding Oadira's hand. "After seeing what happened on the other side of Aarde, where dark water killed the dead sea, if we don't find a way to clear up this dark water, all waterways will be threatened."

"Nier's realm can maintain the presence of dark water as the currents will force it there first before distributing it to all of Aarde's water sources," replied Lyshyla. "If it does distribute out from Nier's realms, the currents will move the acidic, dark waters throughout all of Aarde, killing Aarde slowly. There's enough time to prevent the acidic waters spreading out from Nier's realm in all the water streams."

The river flowed for several miles until they came to an area where the mist grew thin. Oadira was in total shock seeing death all around her on the shores of the river. Skeletons were everywhere, many still chained together in the sand and on the barren ground. She even saw the large, obsidian boulders that many of her kind were tied to so that the ships leaving the Middle Passage could make the weight restrictions, entering the Nautical Trade.

"Swim to the shore so we can rest a bit," Lyshyla urged as she paddled toward land. "None of us have slept in days, and if the mist is lighter here, we may find a safe place to sleep for the night."

Walking up the shores, the devastation was even more obvious. Tens of thousands of skeletons disappeared into the fog. Oadira was struck suddenly by what this scene would have looked like when Sahael fell to Nata's forces. These wouldn't have been sanitary bones littering the ground, but the bodies of men, women, and little children. All dead. All murdered or poisoned by their own land.

Anger swelled in her chest like fire. She hated Natas. That was nothing new. But now she hated all the gods and their machinations. She knew there was a purpose to all of this, but from where she was standing, all she saw were the consequences of protecting Sahael. Why protect it at all if it meant so much suffering.

Lyshyla placed her hand on Oadira's shoulder as if understanding her pain. "My empress," she began. "I know it is hard to see, but there is a purpose here. These bodies could not be taken by the enemy. This land could not be taken. It is more than you or I or the lives of our loved ones. I fear the forces that stand behind Natas are greater and more ruthless than even that demon made flesh. We cannot despair in the face of so much tragedy."

Emotion overcame Oadira. Tears fell from her eyes onto the ground, mingling with a small pool of water from the river. Her tears matched the color of her cerulean eyes. The puddles started to brighten; the dark-blue spots in the water becoming clear.

"Mother," Onika breathed. "Look at the puddle at your feet where your tear landed."

"It's clear!" Ozias gasped. He kneeled down and stuck his finger in it, bringing a few drops to his mouth. He smiled. "It's been cleansed!"

Oadira knelt down to examine the puddle and, sure enough, no acidic tingle burned her finger as she touched it.

"Our tears can clean water?" Onika questioned.

Lyshyla grinned. "No. Look at the Heart."

Oadira glanced down and noticed that Okavango's Heart glowed brighter and brighter suddenly the closer it drew to the cleansed pool.

"Oadira, Okavango's heart is glowing once more. Remove the fifth piece and place it into the bright spot that your tears have created," Lyshyla said.

Oadira removed the piece of Okavango's heart from her necklace, dipping it in her puddle of tears. The dreary, dark-blue, acidic waters transformed into a light blue that spread out from the section Oadira had placed in the waters. The wet ground began to transform, as if the toxins were being absorbed into the rocks and soil. Even the river began to be affected.

"It's absorbing the acid in the Middle Passage waters!" Ozias said.

After several minutes, the waters were transparent, clean, and pure, spreading farther out and into the middle waters of the passage. The renewal from her tears and the piece of Okavango's Heart spread farther and farther out. A light hissing sound could be heard all around as the acid was purged from this section of land. The sound seemed to come from the skeletons all around. It seemed to Oadira that it was the skeletons that were absorbing the poisons. In death, these bones were cleansing the land of toxins, serving Sahael and Alkebulan from the Great Beyond.

Oadira cupped her hands and brought the now fresh water to her lips. The cool liquid immediately soaked into her swollen tongue and soothed her burning throat. She drank more and more, pouring the water over her face and laughing. Ozias ran to the river's edge and jumped in, splashing and drinking freely. Onika did the same with a great splash. Laughter filled the area despite the reminders of death all around them. They were still hungry and so tired, but the clean water lifted their spirits and gave them hope.

More than that. It gave them faith.

Faith was restored to Oadira's heart once again. Just as she had begun to doubt, Ishtar and Obatala had given her a sign of their plans. While still unsure of the grander details to come, Oadira knew she would never question again. Sahael would be redeemed, and with it, the people of Aarde.

Natas would be defeated.

Not today, but someday soon. Of that, she no longer doubted.

"Once these waters are cleaned," Lyshyla said, a laugh to her words, "we can enter through the underground gates, allowing us to swim the rest of the way and taking us deeper into the middle waters. The waters being clean and clear seem to be a permanent fix that will do a lot of good for Sahael. I believe the healed waters will now benefit all Alkebulan because of the currents. We have some distance to swim still. Let's find a place in this area to rest for the night. I know we're all hungry and tired, but there is still a ways to go. We are close, and it will take all we have."

The group followed Lyshyla's advice, finding a cave nearby where the air was clear enough to let their guard down and sleep. After having drunk their fill, Oadira felt refreshed, but appreciated the chance to close her eyes.

The next morning, they swam through the middle waters, finding deep passages into the mountain that lead through dark tunnels. They abandoned themselves to the currents, letting them lead the group where they would. None of them doubted their path now, not even Onika. Ishtar was on their side, and they would let him guide their path through the darkness and cold waters. Luckily the water was now clear and fresh, allowing them to drink freely.

Oadira had no idea what time of day it was, or for how long they had been swimming, but she assumed it had to be late afternoon by the time they arrived at the closed opening of the Sahaedron realm. The four of them floated in a large, underwater cavern with two ten-foot-tall, algae-covered statues of a king and queen. Pale light seemed to come from the water itself, as if bioluminescent algae provided the lamination in shades of green and blue. The left eye on the king's statue and the right eye on the queen's were missing. The doors behind them were obsidian, carved in the royal patterns of Sahael. How this place had been built underwater Oadira couldn't guess. Another testament to the power and skill of the ancient Kemites.

"This is the Nibiru Wall that prevents entry into Sahaedron," Lyshyla said telepathically. *"I've seen carvings of it in Timbuktu. To be here now feels sacred to me."*

"I can see that the eyes on the statues need to be replaced," Oadira replied. *"They're the same color as my eyes and my tattoos. Wait here for my return."*

Oadira swam up to the statue of the king missing its left eye, removing two more pieces from Okavango's Heart around her neck. Only one piece remained. Oadira assumed that the last piece would be the most important of all.

She placed one of the shards in a statue of the king's left eye. Afterward, she swam over to the other statue and placed the seventh piece in the queen's right eye. Oadira rejoined Ozias, Onika, and Lyshyla down at the Nibiru Wall.

The Nibiru Walls in between the two statues of the king and queen retracted into the seafloor, creating a large opening. There was nothing but silence as the water moved slowly past the four of them into the dark opening.

Just as Oadira prepared to swim forward, she thought she heard singing through the water. The sound was haunting, yet beautiful.

"Did you hear that?" Oadira asked.

"Hear what?" Ozias questioned.

"I hear noises coming from the Orishan waters behind us," Oadira said. *"It's almost like singing."*

Through the darkness, Oadira saw points of blue light blinking through the water. Then, into the pale light, swam hundreds of Orishan people emerging from the deep waters of the Middle Passage. Men, women, and children who had chains on their feet, legs, waists, and arms, pulling large boulders with ease.

"What is this?" Onika asked. *"Who are they? They're coming directly at us as if they all want to fight or kill us. What should we do?"*

"Nothing," Lyshyla said calmly.

Oadira eyed the beautiful people who continued approaching her and the royal Family. The people smiled at them through the water. The stones attached to their chains seemed to weigh nothing to them.

"I'm trying to make sense and comprehend what's happening," Oadira whispered telepathically.

"These full-blooded, Black Orishans were once the bodies and skeletons that laid deep beneath the surface of the sea for over four hundred years. This is one of the many reasons you and your family were meant to return to Sahael," Lyshyla said.

Tens of thousands of Orishans filled the cavern, lighting the area with their glowing eyes and tattoos. Even so, it looked as though only a single eye glowed on each person, not two like Oadira and her family. Oadira wondered about it for a second, when Ozias spoke in her mind, pulling her attention back to her family.

"They're just staring at us. Any ideas on what we should do?" Ozias asked.

"We'll remain patient for now," Lyshyla said.

After the Nibiru walls had firmly placed themselves deep into the ground, the eyes of the king and queen on the statues lit up cerulean, matching Oadira's eyes. Suddenly, the water started receding below Sahael's deep-water region, having no effect on the water of the Middle Passage. Soon the cavern emptied and Oadira and the mass of people stood on muddy ground, once again breathing clean air. Water dripped from the ceiling, sounding almost like rain in the massive space.

"Mother, Father, what's going on?" Onika asked.

"I don't know," Ozias whispered.

There was nothing but silence in the air.

"The magic within Okavango's heart is restoring life within Alkebulan, Sahael, and the waters below the river," Lyshyla said as she looked Oadira in the eyes.

The entrance leading into Sahaedron called out to the

people, but no one moved.

"They're just standing there, looking at us with their fierce, sapphire eyes," Ozias said.

"Their eyes are fierce because they died in violence and were resurrected by Okavango's Heart, filling them up with love, hate, and vengeance," Lyshyla said. "As long as Nile's flame burns, their eyes, hearts, and minds will be focused on restoring and rebuilding Sahaedron."

"Wait, they were brought back to life?" Onika asked. "How is that possible?"

"When they died four hundred years ago," Lyshyla answered, "they were blessed to return. Their sacrifice was seen as the truest form of ransom. The tomes in Timbuktu spoke of their return, but I didn't know now was the time. Oh, blessed day!" Tears of joy poured from Lyshyla's eyes as her voice echoed through the cavern. "We see the fulfillment of prophecy in our lifetime! Praise Ishtar and Obatala, Father and Mother of the universe!"

As if hearing Lyshyla's prayer, the statue of the king and queen's eyes emanated in cerulean, where their hands touched, Nile's blue flame erupted in flickers of glowing fire. Smoke from Nile's blue flame spread through the area under the Middle Passage, blessing every one of them with magic to help them cope with their trauma. The vapor smelled like Jasmine on a summer night. Oadira felt suddenly refreshed as if she had just slept for a week and eaten the biggest most satisfying meal in her life. A grin filled Onika's face.

"Now do you trust Lyshyla?" Oadira asked her son.

He laughed. "I don't trust her to tell me anything I actually need to know in advance, but she's doing her best, just like the rest of us."

"Very mature," Ozias said, placing his hand on Onika's shoulder. "You'll make a good king yet one day."

The newly revived people remained in their stationary state, staring at Oadira as the blue mist continued to swirl around them.

"They are waiting for us to move so that they may enter now," Oadira said.

"They are waiting for your command, my queen and empress," Lyshyla said with a nod. "*Their* queen and empress. You wield the power of Okavango. You alone have the power to lead the people." Lyshyla reached over and grasped Okavango's Heart in her hand before holding it up for everyone to see.

The Orishans moved one step closer with their eyes fixated on Okavango's heart.

"I don't understand what's happening," Ozias said.

"Walk to them," Lyshyla said to Oadira.

Oadira walked to the Orishan people slowly, observing them closely. Every man, woman, and child were missing an eye, either the right or left.

"They're missing one eye, right or left, which is why they aren't lit. The sapphire is dark and needs to light them up from within. I know what needs to be done," Oadira said.

The meaning of the scriptures she had read in Iceoth and Timbuktu suddenly made perfect sense to her. Okavango's Heart was never meant to belong to only one person. The power belonged to everyone.

Oadira took another piece of Okavango's heart and said a little prayer in her mind before throwing the gem into the smoky mist from Nile's flame. It ignited in a burst of energy. The power crackled through the smoke like lightning, forking in great tongues of electricity. The energy entered the bodies of every single Orishan present. Instantly, the sapphire eyes of the Orishan people lit up, allowing them the ability to see and move in unison.

"You did it. They can all see now," Ozias said, walking up to be with Oadira as Lyshyla and Onika followed him.

Lyshyla breathed deeply as if a great weight had been removed from her shoulders. "These people will continue to remain here until the currents have completely stopped, ushering in a new beginning of the restored bloodline. We need to enter Sahaedron. For now, at least we know they're safe. We must continue moving."

Mud squished between their toes as Oadira, Osias, Onika, and Lyshyla walked through the dark opening behind the statues. The ground remained wet as they trekked in darkness, but their hearts were light as if guided by joy and thanksgiving. Eventually points of light could be seen along the walls as torches began to light up with blue flames. Carvings covered the walls in reliefs of the crashing of the Kemite ship, the building of Sahael, and the teaching of the people of Aarde.

After another hour, pale sunlight filled the end of the tunnel. They emerged in Sahaedron, one of the great cities of Sahael. Ruined buildings cast shadows in the afternoon light. The deadly fog still lingered like an oppressive weight. A large lake surrounded the city on all sides, crystal and clean from Oadira's use of Okavango's Heart on the waters of Alkebulan. Even with the healed currents, the city lay still and dead, charred bodies here and there along with scattered bones and bleached skulls.

For the first time since she was three years old, Oadira was standing in Sahael.

Her home.

From the maps she had studied over and over again, she

knew that Khartoum Palace where she had lived with her king and queen parents, with her cousins Heziara, Aamira, and Damisiah.

Where were they right now? Each of her chosen sisters had been sent by Solomon on a quest of their own over 30 years ago. Had they been successful? Were they queens in some far-off land? Were they dead and buried, sacrificed by witan enemies, or captured by Natas?

She didn't know. What Oadira did know was that she was standing in Sahael, as had been prophesied. Their journey was ending, but their work was only beginning.

"Let us walk to the center of Sahaedron," Lyshyla said. "There we will find Sahaedron's Keystone. This Keystone allows deep access to Sahaedron when the essence of life and vitality enhancing current flow in Sahael is restored."

"Lead the way, Educator Lyshyla," Onika said with a nod.

They followed Lyshyla through the devastation. Oadira imagined what the great city would have looked like before Natas' assault and bombing. It must have been magnificent and full of light. What a tragedy. Bones continued to litter the ground, some of them still with swords in their backs that had been thrust with such force they had become embedded in the stone walkways and left behind. There were even bones of birds and dogs strewn about; casualties of the Sahaelian failsafe that made it impossible for Natas to take possession of the sacred lands.

Once in the center of Sahaedron, Oadira and her family entered what looked like must have been a plaza at once time. Pillars had fallen and the well-laid stones of the promenade were shattered and cracked by whatever explosives Natas had used all those years ago. There in the center though, intact and unharmed, was the Keystone. It was a large auger made of Orichalcum that had four arms. The Auger held Uluru rock, the largest sapphire gem in Aarde. The stone was four feet across, dingy and lifeless, not reflecting any light penetrating the fog. Its smooth surface was natural and uncut by human hands.

"Uluru's large rock is dead, like many of the Orishans who were once skeletons floating at the bottom of the sea, but now breathe once again," Lyshyla said as she ran her hand across the surface of the massive gemstone. "Many Orishans call it the heartbeat of the sea, with the ability to restore all of what has been lost to Sahael's rivers, lakes, and streams. Oadira, place one of the two remaining pieces of your necklace in the slot on top of Uluru's sapphire."

Oadira nodded and made her way over to the Keystone, placing the second-to-last piece from Okavango's heart into a slot shaped perfectly for the shard.

A great hum emanated from the stone, rattling Oadira's teeth and tingling through her entire body. The sound of rushing waters rumbled through the broken city. The sapphire suddenly lit up and a brightness like that of the sun on a clear spring morning. Oadira covered her eyes to block the light. Shafts of energy swirled around, entering the sky and the ground. The hum continued and Oadira could feel the pebbles and sand at her feet vibrating and bouncing around.

The fog dissipated and pulled into the soil, leaving a blue expanse overhead and a beaming sun in all its glory. Green grass began to poke through the cracks in the stones and a pleasant scent, like blossoms on a summer morning, permeated the land. Several scarred and burned trees burst to life, sprouting leaves and flowers.

Life returned to Sahael as if it had never left.

And most miraculous of all, Oadira noticed the bones all around as fingers of soil, like tree roots, stretched from the earth and contorted around each limb. Muscle and tendon reformed before their very eyes.

“What’s happening to the dead bodies?” Onika asked, pointing as a set of bones quickly became wrapped in muscle and flesh.

“I told you,” Lyshyla smiled. “These bodies and bones couldn’t be taken by Natas and the Ennead. They were promised safety in this life, and they shall have it.”

“Is this happening everywhere in Sahael?” Ozias questioned as more bodies formed and began to move.

“Only here in Sahaedron,” Lyshyla confirmed. “So saith the prophecies.”

All around them, revived people began to stand, fully reborn and healthy. Their dark skin glistened in the sunlight without blemish. As they turned, Oadira noticed their eyes. Much like the Orishans that had been resurrected earlier that day who were each missing an eye, these individuals seemed to have no eyes. Their lids were closed over what appeared to be empty sockets.

“They have no eyes,” Onika whispered as the restored Sahaelians began to look around, murmuring about their blindness.

Lyshyla looked to the sky as a drop of rain hit her forehead. “This too shall be rectified,” she said.

Sapphire rays of light reflected off Uluru’s azure stone as water dripped from a cloudless sky.

“There are no clouds. How is it raining?” Oadira questioned.

In an instant, each drop of water turned into a diamond and bounced on the ground. Ozias shouted and threw his hands over his head to protect himself, but the raining diamonds ceased almost immediately. Even so, thousands of diamonds littered the stone plaza. Lyshyla leaned down and picked one up.

"Oadira," she said. "Do you remember the tales of when you and your cousins were born?"

Looking down at the diamonds and then up at the blind people stumbling about unsure of themselves, Oadira recalled Solomon telling her, Heziara, and Aamira about how the three of them were all born without eyes. Their sockets had been empty, until Solomon had forged new eyes from jewels.

Ozias seemed to realize what Lyshyla meant and immediately began gathering diamonds and handed them to the people blindly circling the Auger.

"Place these gems in your eye sockets," Ozias began shouting.

"They will restore your sight!" Oadira added as she too, along with Onika and Lyshyla, began passing out diamonds to everyone in the area. As the people placed the diamonds in their eyes, the gems lit up blue and their sight returned. Men and women smiled and shouted with joy before grabbing diamonds themselves and helping their families and friends to also regain their sight.

"The Orishan people are now entering in the thousands; they're all placing diamonds into their empty slots," Lyshyla said.

Mobs of Orishans circled the Auger, sharing the diamond pieces among themselves. As the sun set toward the west, more and more revived people could see. The miracle was beyond Oadira's understanding. Healing the land had been one thing, but bringing the people back to life was an entirely different gift. She now understood why the failsafe had destroyed the land.

No. Destroyed was the wrong word.

Preserved.

While to the unfaithful eye Sahael had died in Natas' attack, in truth it had been protected, as had the people. The other cities on the crater were still ruined and lifeless, Oadira now trusted that would only be the case for a short amount of time.

Her sisters were on their own journey right now. They would be watched over the same way she had been until they too returned to Sahael as queens. The people across Aarde would be redeemed.

But as Chima had said just before she sacrificed her life for them to escape the Neutral Zone, there was still work to be done before any victory could even be attempted.

"It'll take some time for the people to restore their right or left eyes," Lyshyla said as the Orishan people drew closer to the Auger.

After having their sight restored, the Sahaelians immediately surrounded Oadira and knelt to show their respect as they chanted the phrase, "*Redder! Redder! Redder!*"

"What are they chanting?" Onika asked.

"They're chanting the word 'savior' in the ancient Sahaelian tongue. They see Oadira as their savior," Lyshyla said.

"My purpose was to bring to pass the immortality and life of the Orishan people," Oadira said. "That was why my sisters and I were born. But no one is saved yet. This part of our journey may be over, but another begins as we attempt to rebuild Sahael and wait for our scattered people to return. Today is a blessing, but we must remember that not everyone will have the gift of being brought back to life. Some sacrifices, like Chima and others, will be rewarded not in this life, but in the next."

"Yes, Lyshyla grinned. "But you've made it possible for your people to return home. They will travel deep to the Sahaedron realm, heading here. While the dead continue to rest in other parts of Alkebulan, I feel that the toxic fogs and poisoned waters have been healed throughout Sahael. All that remains is the final shard of Okavango's heart-shaped sapphire necklace hanging from your neck. You've used nine of the smaller ten pieces to help restore life-magic to the people and to Sahael's realm. We need to find out what that last piece is for."

Oadira remained silent for a moment as she made eye contact with Lyshyla.

"This place is the home that I've always wanted," Oadira admitted. "Yet it doesn't feel like home. My children are spread out all over Aarde with the same yearning for home that I share. I long for their return to the holy land of their ancestors."

After Oadira finished speaking, she looked around and saw the Orishans circling the south end of the plaza and singing a song in a language she didn't understand.

"What are they doing over there?" Onika asked.

Lyshyla stepped forward and blinked several times as if trying to believe what she was seeing.

Suddenly a loud hum, not unlike what Uluru's Rock had produced, emanated from the ground where the Orishans were singing. Large rectangular stones began extending from the ground, reaching twelve feet into the air before they stopped.

"Are those…" Oadira gasped.

"The Nairohenge Gates are now operational," Lyshyla breathed.

The family ran forward through the crowd until they stood before the gates. Energy tingled on the air and Oadira knew that the portals the Nairohenge could open would take them throughout Aarde. Suddenly the thought of rescuing millions of enslaved people filled Oadira with joy.

"And somewhere among the people who were brought back to life, there must be navigators," Ozias said.

"Yes, many," Lyshyla confirmed. "This place is the go-between of Aarde and Sahaedron. Every enslaved Black that was killed or chose death rather than bondage could come here for a second chance at redemption. They were all killed by witans who wanted to enslave them and take their culture away through the whitewashing process. These sets of Nairohenge Gates need to be activated. A power source is needed if we want to get inside the capital city of Sahael itself."

As Onika walked among the Nairohenge stones, energy began crackling from the rocks and striking his arms and throat.

"Onika!" Oadira shouted. "Come back here! We don't know what power---"

A flash of light encompassed Onika. He started scratching his throat as it began to light up in cerulean to match his eyes and tattoos. The Auger holding the stone of Uluru glowed as well, shooting a shaft of azure light into the sky. Onika turned and looked at the Keystone, confusion evident on his face. He continued scratching his throat as he started coughing, letting out a shout directly at the stone of Uluru that enhanced the indicolite rays of light. He opened his mouth and a shout emanated from his vocal cords that shook the ground. It wasn't a harsh sound, but more of a call that vibrated every cell in Oadira's body.

They knew when he was born that Onika had been given the gift of shout.

Now she understood what that meant.

The crowd's diamond eyes filled with blue light, tattoos glowing brightly. A peace fell over the crowd. For the first time, Oadira understood the meaning of true Sahaelian royalty.

"He is definitely the high king of Sahael," Lyshyla said as Onika's shout ended, and he smiled at them sheepishly. "His gift of shout alone gives him the title."

Oadira looked around at her people. "The Nairohenge

Gates have risen. Onika's shout was the power needed to activate the gates, allowing us to use them once we get to Khartoum Palace."

"By my count, four of the nineteen gates are operational," Ozias counted. "But without the gates in Khartoum Palace active, there is nowhere to travel without Navigators and Gate Guardians. We'll have to swim up through the Sahaelian waters to arrive in Sahael."

"Let us rest for the night," Lyshyla said, looking at the setting sun. "Tomorrow we can reassess our options. After today though, I think we've earned a moment of peace where we don't have to think about anything beyond this moment."

Morning came all too quickly.

Fruit trees had returned to bloom and the family ate a breakfast of fresh apples, peaches and berries while sitting in the ruined plaza on what remained of a palace wall. Birds flew overhead as if they'd never left, while a deer ran through the plaza completely unafraid of the humans hauling stones and debris on their backs. Workers had already started clearing rubble on Oadira's orders, along with the skeletons of the Narsan and Ennead soldiers that had not been resurrected with the Orishans. Songs of joy and thanksgiving continually echoed on the warm breeze.

"We'll have to find another way into Sahael since we've bypassed the safety mechanisms," Oadira replied, chewing on a juicy slice of peach.

"There are multiple ways to enter Sahael," Lyshyla said.

"We can do that through the lakes, rivers, or ponds. There are no gates to pass through. We are inside the crater, so making it to the other cities, including Sahael itself, is just a matter of time and effort. We need to travel and come up through the large bodies of water, entering Sahael from Sahaedron, and emerge on the other side from Lake Sahael. We can arrive from the water on to dry land. Although we have restored the connection to Sahaedron, it seems that this place is still full of division. I feel it needs to be unified."

"But the people seem so happy," Onika said, drinking fresh water from a cracked goblet he found in the ruins. "I don't see any divisions."

"Sahael and Alkebulan fell from within long before Natas attacked," Lyshyla said as she stood up from her rocky seat. "You remember the lessons, Onika. The politics of this place had become tainted with hate and distrust. Such dynamics are likely to reassert themselves now that these people have been revived. They have a cause to work toward now in rebuilding their city to its former glory, but glory has a way of igniting the worst in people, and these are the same people who allowed Sahael to morally rot in the first place."

"Perhaps we should stay and figure out what's going on," Oadira said.

"In time, you'll have the opportunity to do that, but for right now, it is imperative that you all get to Sahael," Lyshyla urged. "You are so close. All we have to do is follow the current. That should take us to the Orishan courtyard inside of Khartoum Palace."

"Any objections?" Oadira asked as she smiled at her husband.

"We've come this far," he chuckled. "What's one more swim? Plus, I've always dreamed of exploring Sahael and the crater lands. Swimming the waters between Sahaedron and Khartoum Palace will be a dream come true."

After finishing their meal, Oadira and her family spread the word they would be swimming to Khartoum Palace and for the people to continue clearing debris and gathering stores of food. They had no idea when they would return but hoped it would be in a few days at most. Lyshyla led the royals to a beach on the lakeshore and pointed to the southeast.

"We'll swim to the river inlet south of the lake," she informed. "It should be a fairly pleasant journey, unlike most of our other swims over the past few months."

They dove in and breathed freely of the clean water. Fish swam around as beds of kelp reached toward the sun. Life had returned to the waters as well as the land, and Oadira was overcome with gratitude at how fully Alkebulan had been healed in a single day.

The four of them swam from the lake to the in-between passing, following the current for several miles. On Lyshyla's command, they surfaced and gazed up at a ruined city much like Sahaedron, with crumbling towers and burned buildings. Surprisingly, as they swam closer, the water grew shallower and shallower, until at the edge of Sahael, the river water dried up completely. They stepped not onto muddy ground, but parched and cracked dirt that looked as if it hadn't seen rain in decades.

"Did the river always dry up here?" Ozias asked as he kicked at the arid soil, sending a plume of dust into the air.

"It…didn't," Lyshyla said after a brief pause. "The Orishan courtyard is just ahead. Let's walk to the docks and find our way to the central palace. I'm not sure what's going on."

The courtyard was cloaked in death as the family set foot on the stone shore of the docks. Dead Sahaelian knights and

Narsan soldiers were everywhere in skeleton form; the enclosure itself flooded with debris. Bodies hung from the blanched and decaying Marula Trees slumping out of what once had been the inner lake inside of the Orishan courtyard. The dry ponds were littered with burned leaves and dead grass. Corpses of Narsan soldiers, carcasses of Lope Mastiffs, and Nitrate bomb pieces littered the ground.

Blackened walls stood crumbling on the southern end of what had once been a well-tended garden, now gray and lifeless. This had been her home as a child. Few memories remained of this palace and its surrounding gardens, but Oadira could almost place herself here among the flowers playing with her cousins when the bombs started dropping and her mother grabbed the three girls and ran them to safety.

"Why are all the plants here still dead?" Onika asked as he plucked a brittle leaf from a withered tree branch. "I thought when we healed Sahaedron, plant life across the continent was revived. Not the people of course, like you said, but at least the grass and things."

Lyshyla walked over to a stone basin littered with dead leaves. She rubbed her hand against the interior of the large bowl, pulling away with ash and dust on her palm.

"There's no water anywhere around," she said, looking to the sky. "It's as if all the water has been removed from this city."

"Was that something Natas might have done?" Ozias asked. "It didn't seem natural how the river dried up on the borders of the city."

"It's a distinct possibility," Lyshyla nodded. "Nata wanted the bloodlines dead and the princesses as well. When he wasn't able to find the princesses, I can see him doing whatever he could to scar this place and remove any chance of its revival, even through the ancient healing magic. There is no water in Sahael."

They continued walking, looking for any sign of water, and found none. Everywhere else they had been on Alkebulan, water had been plentiful; poisoned and toxic yes, but plentiful. Once healed, the water had given life to the land. Here in Sahael though, the dryness permeated every stone and patch of earth.

Whatever Natas had done to curse this place, he had been incredibly effective.

"That's what remains of Khartoum Palace," Lyshyla said, pointing to the fragmented walls with their soot-covered exterior. "It was beautiful once. A place of wisdom and music."

"This is worse than in Sahaedron," Ozias said, scanning the entire plaza.

"It's like no life can return here," Onika agreed.

"It's because there is no water to grant that life." Lyshyla's shoulders slumped. "Natas was effective in ruining Sahael even after his forces retreated when the land became poisoned."

Oadira stepped forward, gazing at the destroyed palace walls. "Tell me what happened here."

"You know what happened here," Lyshyla replied.

"Tell me again," Oadira said. She wanted to feel it while standing in this place, standing in Sahael, in what would have been her lifelong home. She wanted to feel the anger and frustration at a life that had been taken from her and millions of other people all because of hubris and tyranny.

"The Narsans with their floating airships dropped Nitrate obsidian bombs on all four sections of Khartoum Palace," Lyshyla said slowly. "They then deployed the Narsan troops to help clear out the halls and kill any members of the four royal families of Sahael, the four pharaohs and Ptolemies of Egyptus, and representatives of the Horn of Alkebulan."

"Let's go inside what remains of my home," Oadira stated. "Keep recounting what happened. We all need to be reminded, now more than ever."

Oadira, Ozias, and Onika followed Lyshyla into the Sahaelian Commons, seeing the skeletons of dead royals that had been mangled by Natas's hounds. The ceiling had long since caved in and one of NeRu's eyes had been destroyed.

"Lord Commander Natas spared no resources, wanting to sever the lineages of the three great empires of Alkebulan," Lyshyla continued as she climbed over what had once been ceiling stones.

They followed Lyshyla down the Orishan Halls to the center of Khartoum Palace as she continued the requested tale.

"These are those who were here before us, the Sahaelians who died at the hands of the Ennead Legion. They died because Khartoum Palace was caught off guard by an unlikely force who allowed White Darkness into the hearts of those posing as allies to infiltrate and attack Sahael from the skies."

They walked through the center of Khartoum Palace, where the Nabtahenge Gates had retracted into the ground. Several tapestries lay burned and weathered beside what remained of an ivory wall with a Marula Tree carved into the face. A flash of memory hit Oadira. She could have sworn she had walked through this wall while in her mother's arms. Cracks ran along the surface, but the stone itself was still intact. Oadira ran her finger along one of the carved tree limbs. As she did so, pale blue light trickled like water across the surface of the engraving. Her eyes and tattoos immediately reacted, lighting up as well.

"What's happening?" Onika asked.

The stone split in two down the middle of the tree and pulled apart, opening on a dusty staircase.

"I've been here before," Oadira whispered.

She descended the stairs into a dark basement area. Ozias found torches on the walls and used his Orishan artes to light them. The room at the bottom of the carved stairway was large, bathed in Ozias' flickering fire light. A fire pit acted as the centerpiece to the sanctuary, while old tapestries still hung on the walls. Several chairs lay toppled beside the pit. Other than that, the room was empty and seemed fairly undisturbed. The ceiling was intact, and to Oadira's eyes it seemed no one had been in or out in the 50 years since the attack.

Forcing herself, Oadira turned to her right where she had left her mother's dying form lying against the wall. A large reddish-black bloodstain marred the wall and floor, but her mother's remains were nowhere to be found in the secret hiding place.

"My mother's body isn't here," Oadira said sadly as she looked around the room. "It should be here. She was there," Oadira pointed at the crimson stain. "She had me cut her throat so that the protective powers of her love could keep me safe until I stood here again."

Oadira began to weep; tears streaming down her face. Her sobs echoed through the cavernous room.

This is where it all began. This is where it all ended.

"I'm sorry," Oadira gasped as she wiped her eyes. Ozias came to her, throwing his arms around her in a tight and loving embrace.

What had happened to her mother's body? Had Natas taken it, desecrated her corpse in his anger?

She didn't know.

She may never know.

“There has to be an explanation why her body isn’t here. Perhaps Solomon can provide us with some answers,” Lyshyla said.

“No one has seen Solomon since my mom was like my age,” Onika said.

Lyshyla smiled. “That doesn’t mean he’s not working toward the good of all people. We will see him again. I promise. Come, let’s continue exploring. There is much we still need to learn.”

The group left the hidden sanctuary and stepped back into the sunlight streaming through the fallen ceilings. They walked to the center where the Nabtahenge Gates remained below the ground in Khartoum Palace.

“You can see these empty troughs here,” Lyshyla said, pointing to stone canals in the floor about a foot wide that ran like small rivers through the palace. “The waters aren’t running through Khartoum Palace, preventing life from rejuvenating the halls once more and activating the Nabtahenge Gates. Running water is needed to flow through Khartoum Palace to help restore life, magic, hope, and power.”

“Most of the canals are covered in debris and broken,” Ozias shrugged. “Even if we could get water flowing from somewhere, it’s not going to be able to reach the gates to activate anything.”

“We’re here in Sahael, a place in ruins and cursed with no water even while the rest of the land now thrives. There is nothing here,” Oadira said in frustration as she shook her head and flailed her arms.

“There is a waterfall in Sahael that feeds into every lake, ocean, pond, river, and stream. It runs through Sahael and touches each body of water in all of Aarde. Those waters may be able to tell the story," Lyshyla said.

"If they're still flowing at all," Ozias replied.

"Then that's where we'll go," Onika said with a smile.

"I thought you were tired of walking and traveling," Ozias grinned, nudging his son playfully.

"That was before I saw thousands of people brought back to life in front of my face," Onika chuckled. "I'm not quite as worried about things now; water or no water."

Lyshyla urged them all to follow her as they walked through the front gates of Khartoum Palace through the debris and rubble outside.

Ozias held his hand over his eyes to block the sun as he scanned Sahael's broken city landscape. "Everything is dead. The grass is yellow, the trees are withering away, and the bodies of water are all dry and empty. Everything seems to be void of all life. There don't seem to be any animals in Sahael either."

They walked to the waterfall behind Khartoum Palace. As they feared, it was no longer running. Not even a drip of moisture fell from the cliffs above.

"Without water, Sahael can't grow, people can't eat or grow crops, and the animals can't reproduce," Lyshyla said as she pointed to the edge of the waterfall. "Nassir's sapphire obelisk blesses the currents and the waters that flow throughout all Sahael, moving through Khartoum Palace. Perhaps Natas did something to the monument."

"Where is the obelisk?" Ozias asked.

"In the grove to the east," Lyshyla answered. "Follow me."

They entered what at one time would have been a magnificent grove of Marula Trees, flowers, and trimmed bushes. Now it was a skeletal mass of twisting branches baking in the sun.

In the center of the garden stood what remained of a blue sapphire stone obelisk that Oadira assumed at one time had to have been twelve feet tall. It now had been broken in half at about only seven feet. The remainder of the obelisk lay half-buried in the ground a few feet away.

Lyshyla crouched on the crisp yellow grass next to the broken section and ran her fingers over a series of gemstones that had been smashed and shattered in their housings. All the carvings had also been destroyed, with hammer and hatchet marks evident across the surface. One large indentation dented the front side near the top, sending cracks webbing in all directions.

"The obelisk has been cursed," Lyshyla breathed, head low. "Not only did they mar the exterior, but there are also runes scratched here and here of Nata's writing. This is the black arte of Khalidah, used by Natas himself. The obelisk was meant to bless the waters of Sahael, but Natas tainted it, leading to this ruined place that even the healing magic of Ishtar and Obatala can't touch."

A dry wind blew as they stood there silently. Dead tree limbs creaked. Stiff grass crunched beneath Lyshyla's knees. This couldn't be it. They had come so far and sacrificed so much. Alkebulan lived again! The people of Sahaedron had been resurrected to help in the coming gathering and rebuilding. And now, after all that, Natas has succeeded in undermining the gods not by poisoning or killing, but by simply removing the water.

Lyshyla quietly cried next to the broken obelisk. Ozias and Onika stood by, looking at the ground.

Oadira stared at the crystalline blue stone. So far, everything the gods had planned anciently for this time had come to pass. The princesses had been born and protected. Oadira had married an heir of Sahael, she had four sons destined to become kings. Three of them had been betrothed to princesses and would rule as prophesied.

So how could it all fall apart now?

How could Natas win?

While staring at the broken obelisk, Odira noticed something about the large chip near the top. The cut was four inches long, and at least an inch deep. It looked to have been caused by an ax swung with incredible force. The gash was deeper than all the others and would have required an orichalcum blade, or one conjured by Khalidah magic. Whoever had hit the obelisk with that blow had to have been massive, and far stronger than normal men. It had likely been that blow that broke the obelisk in the first place.

There was only one person Oadira could think of who had that kind of strength, fueled by rage and hate.

Natas.

Natas himself had broken this ancient artifact. It had been his blow that left behind the prominent, deep scar in the stone. His loathing for Sahael had been enough to curse the land.

Oadira kneeled beside Lyshyla as the Educator wiped tears from her eyes. Reaching out, Oadira placed her fingers in the gash Natas had left behind. It was deep and jagged, shaped almost like a gemstone.

A loud gasp filled Oadira's chest.

"What is it?" Ozias asked, stepping forwards as if worried for his wife.

Oadira didn't speak. She reached up to the final remaining piece of Okavango's Heart still hanging by the chain around her neck. She removed it and held the shard a few inches above Natas' rageful strike.

It would fit perfectly.

Natas, in his fury, hate, and thoughtless selfishness, had created the very means for reviving Sahael that the gods knew would be needed when the sun first rose over Aarde millennia before. Okavango's Heart, giver of life, could theoretically be placed in the slot and erase the curse Natas had placed on the blessing stone. Would it work? Oadira couldn't be sure, but something told her Ishtar and Obatala, in the mother and father gods' wisdom, had known Natas would seal his own fate no matter what he did.

In the end, Natas' enmity for Sahael would be its salvation.

"This gash," Oadira said. "It is the same shape as the final piece of Okavango's Heart. The blade that left this cut behind unknowingly has saved Sahael."

"Will it work?" Onika asked excitedly.

Oadira looked at her son and smiled. "The gods knew all of this would happen, and they allowed a way for us to save ourselves." She turned to Lyshyla. "What are your thoughts?"

Glancing from the gemstone to the abrasion in the broken monument, Lyshyla's cheek twitched. "I don't know. There has never been anything written about this. There is no prophecy that mentions anything about a ninth stone in Okavango's Heart, and yet there were nine stones. Nygaard's prophecy was clear."

"No prophecy is clear," Ozias chuckled. "If you haven't learned that truth, Educator Lyshyla, then you haven't learned anything. I say place the stone in the cut and see what happens."

Lyshyla grabbed Oadira's hand before she could place the blue stone in the slash. "We don't know what will happen if you place that gem in the obelisk. I don't know what will happen. It could heal things, or it could do something else completely unknown. And if it does work, the currents will continue to lead everyone to Sahael. Are you ready for that?"

Pulling her hand slowly from Oadira's, Lyshyla nodded toward the broken obelisk lying in the dirt. "Everything that happens from here on out will be beyond anyone's control and understanding."

Oadira placed Okavango's last piece into Nassir's obelisk. The gem glowed blue as tendrils of azure energy filled the cracks along the obelisk like fingers reaching for something. The energy trickled along the sides and into the ground.

An earthquake shook the area. Dust lifted into the air, and Ozias coughed. Oadira and Lyshyla stood up as Aarde itself seemed to shake asunder.

Ouzoud's Waterfall exploded with a loud roar as water poured over the precipice. Liquid began to seep up through the caked soil, turning the dried dirt into vibrant, dark mud.

"Water!" Ozias cheered.

The air grew moist and humid. The parched grass turned green and soft. Leaves burst into bloom on the trees surrounding them.

Sahael breathed back to life. The dead skeletons, while not returned to life like those of Sahaedron, seemed to sink into the ground, as if Aarde itself offered them an honorable burial. What moments before had been a depressing desert now sprang to life in shades of green and flowering blossoms.

"Sahael lives!" Lyshyla cried. She seemed to relax, shoulders dropping slightly. Her face softened. "So much work and time. So much suffering. May the gathering begin."

Oadira felt as alive as the city of Sahael. She was once again standing in her homeland, where she had been born. All the trials and years of waiting had paid off. She remembered the words of the giant man Ogum just before he gave her Okavango's Heart. "The gods lay out a path, but it is up to each of us to choose to walk it. You may think you're the first person to set out on this quest. You're not. You're simply the first to choose to come this far and not give up. That makes you special in my eyes."

She hadn't given up. Ozias hadn't given up. Her sons hadn't given up. Lyshyla hadn't given up.

And now Sahael lived once more.

A bright light suddenly shot into the sky from the direction of the ruins of Khartoum Palace. The blue shaft reached into the stratosphere like a beacon.

"What is that?" Onika asked, pointing at the mysterious light.

A large grin spread across Lyshyla's face. "I think I know. Follow me."

They made their way back to Khartoum Palace through the same doors they exited, climbing over the debris once again. Water flowed through the troughs, spilling out in places where chunks of rubble damaged the stone rivers. There at the center of Khartoum Palace, the Nabtahenge Gates had risen from out of the ground. The large rectangular stones had pushed aside tons of rubble during their ascent, and now stood proudly, crackling with blue energy. Wind blew from the Gate. The beacon light was blinding. Oadira held her hand in front of her eyes to block the piercing shimmer.

The tower of light slowly dimmed and Oadira looked more closely at the Gate. In the center of the stones swirled a portal similar to what she had seen in Neir's Realm when they had left for the western lands. A shadow appeared in the center and grew more opaque, taking the shape of a man.

"There's a man in the center of Nabtahenge," Onika said, pointing at the man in a black, hooded robe in between the four single Nabta Gates.

The being then stepped out of the portal with two other men by his side before removing his hood. The lead individual was bald, dark skin glistening in the Gate's power. His blue and purple robes swished in the breeze.

Oadira recognized him immediately, even though it had been almost 35 years since she had seen him.

"Solomon!" Lyshyla shouted. She clambered down the pile of rubble toward Solomon, almost tripping in her excitement. She embraced Solomon, almost knocking him over. Oadira could hear the man chuckle as he patted the Educator's back.

A broad smile filled Oadira's face. It was done. Solomon was here.

Ozias took her hand and they followed Lyshyla to the scarred floor of Khartoum Palace. Onika walked close behind. As they approached, Solomon pulled from Lyshyla's embrace and bowed slightly to the royal family.

"I am that I am," Solomon said, placing his hands together in front of his chest as if about to pray. "The Times are upon us, and time is against us. Your house isn't in order. There is division in Sahaedron already, and it must be resolved as soon as possible,"

"I have so many questions that need answering," Oadira said as she fixated on Solomon's glowing blue eyes.

"I know, Oadira," Solomon nodded. He motioned toward his two companions. "Before you speak, let me introduce your new navigator and Midjay Gate guardian. They have been trained in the old ways and will keep this gate fully functional for the good of the people of Aarde. Now, as I said before, your realm is out of order and must be united first. Once your kingdom is ordered, I will answer the questions you have. That's my solemn promise. Even though you return to your respective kingdom, there must always be a high king in Sahael. Your son, Onika, must stay."

"I don't understand," Oadira said as she looked to Lyshyla for answers. "We're here in Sahael to stay together and await the reunion of our people. Our sons will be arriving with their betrothals."

"Why would Onika have to stay but not Oadira and myself?" Ozias asked. "We've come all this way. It's time for us and Lyshyla to rebuild Sahael."

"Professor Lyshyla's work is done," Solomon said. "It was her responsibility to protect you and your family for the last thirty years and get you to Sahael to help you stop the events. Your actions have made Sahael a threat to what hides in the shadows. You have set in motion the Gathering. Soon, your sisters will arrive, who will be presented with the same tasks of getting their kingdoms in order before we deal with the real threats that plague your people."

"You're responsible for what happens from here on out," Lyshyla said, stepping away from Ozias and Oadira to be next to Solomon. She reached out her hand toward the prince. "Onika, this is your choice and your destiny. You are the High King of Sahael. Your place is here, but your parents must go back to Sahaedron to unite a divided people."

Oadira stepped forward. "No! I'm not losing all of my sons. I've sacrificed too much to have to leave Onika too and help unite a people I don't even know. I'm tired and I want to rest!"

Her shout echoed through what remained of Khartoum Palace. Tears came to her eyes. What did all this mean? She had thought they would arrive in Sahael and begin rebuilding as the Diaspora began to gather. What was Solomon implying? That they would be forced out of Sahael to serve somewhere else? What had it all been for?

Solomon stepped closer to Oadira. A small smile touched his lips, but she could see his sadness in the lines around his eyes.

Compassion and understanding flowed from the man. He wrapped his arms around her and a calm embrace. Immediately, Oadira began weeping, as if his very presence told her it was okay to let go. Emotions surged from her with every sob. Solomon held her close, patting her back.

"It's alright," Solomon whispered. "You have done so much for so many. Your efforts will echo long after this life. There will be few people in Aarde ignorant of your name." Solomon broke the hug and looked into Oadira's eyes. "I know you thought coming to Sahael would mean peace and rest for you and your family. But look around. Life has returned, and the people of Sahaedron live once more as prophesied, but the divisions that existed persist even now. Your work is only beginning. Sahael requires that your kingdoms be put in order before taking on the greater burdens of Aarde. And yes, there are greater burdens to come."

"What if I don't want to shoulder them?" Oadira asked.

Solomon grinned broadly. "That is not who you are, Oadira Ocnus, Queen of Iceoth, Empress of Neir's Realm, Ruler of Sahael. You've proven that again and again. Even so, the choice is yours. If you wish to remain here in quiet and peace, leaving your people's fate to others, then I will allow it."

Oadira turned and looked at her husband. Ozias chuckled and glanced from the ground up to Oadira. His laugh brought a smile to her face.

Ozias knew what she would choose.

Oadira knew it too.

Her path was not one of quiet and docility. She was a queen of action and service. Life had not turned out how she would have chosen, which was a good thing. Or maybe she had chosen it. After all, when challenges were presented, she chose to face them. Had she truly wanted a life of ease on a plantation, she could have had that 30 years ago.

No. Oadira wanted the good of all people, and if that meant adapting and serving, she would do it.

“What do we need to do?” she asked Solomon.

“Return to Sahaedron,” he smiled. “Leave Sahael to us. Begin rebuilding the city and wait for others to arrive. Your main problem will be the people who have been resurrected. The task before you will not be easy. I already sense divisions reasserting themselves, and the people have only been revived for a day. They are proud and selfish. You must prepare them to serve. Teach them to trust in faith as you do, and I promise soon you’ll be reunited with your four sons. I am Solomon, the Protector of Aarde, and I give you my word.”

Oadira’s heart raced as butterflies danced in her stomach. “I thought our journey would be over once we reached Sahael but fell now it is only beginning.”

“No journey truly reaches its end until our bodies are laid in the ground,” Lyshyla said. “Your journey will be no different.”

Ozias took Oadira’s hand. “I guess we’re going to Sahaedron to rebuild and await the coming people.”

“Yes,” Oadira agreed. She turned to Solomon. “What of my cousins? Where are Heziara, Aamira, and Damisiah?”

“Your sisters are on their journey to Sahael too,” Solomon answered. “The gods are on their side, just as they have been with you. I have no doubt their tales will be as thrilling as yours, and your reunion sweet.” Solomon turned and pointed at the glowing Gates. “The portal will return you to Sahaedron. Work there with the people and prepare. Your rest will be short, but your glory beyond description. I will see you again when you least expect.”

Oadira hugged Solomon again, before doing the same with

Lyshyla. Onika embraced his mother tightly.

"I'll be okay," he said in her ear.

"I know you will, High King of Sahael," Oadira replied.

She turned with Ozias and walked toward the gateway. The air tingled around her as energy crackled and pulsed. In a few moments she would be in Sahaedron again, shepherding a people she barely understood. One day soon her sisters would arrive, and Aarde would shake before their power. The enslaved people would go free. Natas and his armies would be wiped out. Peace would spread throughout the world as promised.

But for now, the work commenced.

And Oadira was okay with that.

They had made it to Sahael after all these years. Their visit would be brief, but nothing more than that had ever been promised to them.

With her husband's hand in hers, they walked through the portal.

She turned to him and smiled. "We will do what we must."

Ozias smiled back. "As long as you're by my side, nothing can stop us."

The light encased them as they stepped into their future.

THE END

www.ingramcontent.com/pod-product-compliance
Lightning Source LLC
Chambersburg PA
CBHW010448310726
48979CB00018B/2857/J

* 9 7 8 1 9 6 3 0 8 9 0 4 2 *